I0623522

True Love

New Adult Sweet Romance Series, Volume 7

Ellie J. Adams

Published by Wheelhouse Publishers LLC, 2020.

Copyright

True Love: A New Adult Sweet Romance
New Adult Romance Series, Book 7
by Ellie J. Adams
A Wheelhouse Publishers paperback edition.

This title was originally published as *True Love* (Sweet Romance edition) / *Forbidden Passion* (Steamy Romance edition) by E.J. Adams. Copyright 2014 by E.J. Adams Romance.

Wheelhouse Publishers, LLC
c/o Registered Agents, Inc.
82 Wendell Avenue, Suite 100
Pittsfield, MA 01201
To learn more about Wheelhouse Publishers, visit:
wheelhousepublishers.com

CHAPTER 1

Amanda Evans

The alarm on my phone rang for the third time. I'd already hit snooze twice. Time to drag myself out of bed and face the day. I needed to start going to bed earlier.

I reached my arm out from under the covers and felt around for my phone. When I found it, I pulled it under the covers, slid the unlock button and turned off the alarm.

I threw the sheets off of my head and rolled over onto my back. A breeze from the ceiling fan swept across me. I pushed the covers the rest of the way off and climbed out of bed.

The floor was cool as my feet met the wood. I stood and padded across the bedroom to my bathroom. I was thankful that I didn't have any classes until the afternoon. It would probably take me until lunch to feel like I was fully ready to engage with the world.

I was in the fifth year of my doctoral program. The first three years I took classes and my preliminary exams. The last two years have been devoted to researching and writing my doctoral dissertation. I teach some introductory undergraduate courses in the Classics department. The teaching covers my tuition and offers a small stipend for living expenses.

I looked at myself in the bathroom mirror. The bags under my eyes weren't nearly as bad as I felt they were. My hair, however, was an entirely different matter. I also had a wicked crick in my neck.

"How Sweet it Is" by James Taylor rang from my phone, telling me it was my boyfriend, Brad, calling.

"Hey," I answered.

"Good morning, beautiful," Brad's voice greeted me. "You free for lunch?"

"As long as I'm done in time for my two o'clock class."

"How about twelve thirty?"

"See you then."

"Great. Gotta run or I'll be late for my finance class."

"See you at in a few hours."

We ended our call, and I smiled. A sweet surprise as I didn't think Brad would have time to meet for lunch today.

He and I had been dating for the past year. We met through his sister, who is in the Master's program in the Classics department. Otherwise, it was hard to imagine our paths would ever have crossed.

Brad was a graduating senior who had been a star wide receiver for the USC Trojans. Brad was also a business major, but he told me the degree was to help him know how to invest all the money he was going to make in the National Football League. He had been drafted in the second round and would report to training camp later in the summer. I figured that was where our relationship would end. We hadn't discussed it, but I think we both knew we weren't destined to be together beyond his senior year.

Neither one of us had been looking for anything too serious. He was training to start his career in the NFL. I was preparing to defend my dissertation and find a teaching position for the following academic year.

Brad and I were polar opposites, but there had been an undeniable mutual attraction when we met. I must admit that I assumed the worst stereo type about him as a dumb jock. To be fair, he also assumed that I was just a nerdy bookworm.

I am a nerdy bookworm. It kinda goes with studying the Classics. But I also have a fun and adventurous side. I learned Brad is very smart. An Academic All American in addition to being one of the top college football players in the country.

We hit it off, went out on a few dates, and have been together since. We agreed not to think about any future together beyond the academic year. It has worked well for us. Neither of us has seen any reason to upset the apple cart.

I showered, dressed, and followed the aroma of freshly brewed coffee coming from the kitchen. I poured myself a cup and made my first decision of the day: plain or cinnamon raisin bagel? I decided on cinnamon raisin. I pulled a bagel out of the package and placed it into the toaster. I took a sip of coffee, walked over to the kitchen table, and sat down and opened the student newspaper.

There was an interview with Brad and the other USC football players who were going to the NFL. Brad liked to joke around, but he was pretty humble. He hadn't mentioned the interview to me. I thought his comments were the best, but I am biased. He talked about how fortunate he was to have an opportunity to make an NFL team.

The toaster dinged. I got up and crossed the kitchen. I spread a little butter on the bagel and went back to the table. The smell of warm cinnamon and raisins filled the kitchen. It blended with the scent of mocha coffee. *Ah*, I thought.

After eating I put my breakfast dishes in the dishwasher and poured a second cup of coffee and went to get the papers I still needed to finish grading for my afternoon class. I had just put the pile of papers on the living room coffee table when my cell phone dinged.

Glancing at the text message I was glad I had already eaten, or this would have ruined my appetite. I was hoping that it wasn't an omen for how the rest of my day was going to go.

CHAPTER 2

Matteo Rosetti

Matteo Rosetti was editing the footage that he had filmed earlier in the day. He was working on the final film of his master's in film study at Centro Sperimentale di Cinematografia (Experimental Cinema Center)—Italy's national film school. Matteo was also going to submit the film as his entry into the Pacific Coast Pictures film contest. The winner received a film making internship at Pacific Coast Pictures in Hollywood and a scholarship to participate in post-graduate workshops at the University of Southern California (USC) School of Cinematic Arts.

Matteo was one of the top film students in his program and considered a leading candidate to win the contest. He had received a world class education in film at Centro Sperimentale di Cinematografia, one of the world's best film schools. But Matteo wanted to add to his education through the workshops at USC, another of the world's best film schools, and be in the heart of movie making in Hollywood. Matteo dreamed of being the next great film director.

Matteo felt the arms of his girlfriend drape over his shoulders. She kissed him on his neck. Francesca Parisi was an Italian beauty. She had a near perfect figure, long dark hair, flawless olive skin, and stunning brown eyes.

"Take me to dinner," said Francesca.

"I need to finish these edits," replied Matteo.

"But I'm hungry," she said with a pout.

"I'm sorry, but you know I must get this done tonight to make the contest entry deadline."

"Contest, contest, contest. That is all you can talk about."

"You know how important this is to me."

"What about me? Aren't I important to you?"

"Yes, of course you are."

"Don't you love me?"

"Yes, I love you."

Matteo did love Francesca. In a way. He'd known her his entire life. He had dated her almost as long. Their families were very close, and it was assumed, and expected, that Matteo and Francesca would get married one day.

Matteo just wasn't sure he was *in love* with Francesca. But he wasn't going to debate the issue with her. And he certainly wasn't going to question the assumption that he and Francesca would marry each other one day. Neither family would tolerate anything other than Matteo Rosetti and Francesca Parisi joining in Holy Matrimony.

Matteo figured he could do worse than Francesca for a wife. She was, after all, one of the most beautiful girls he had ever met. She had few interests and was pretty self-centered, but she could be fun. They did have some good times together.

"Please. Just let me finish editing this one scene. Just thirty more minutes. Then we can go to dinner," Matteo said.

"If you truly loved me you would drop everything and take me to dinner," Francesa replied as she stomped across the room.

She can be such a child, Matteo thought. But he had not time for an argument.

"Thirty minutes," repeated Matteo. "Then we can go to dinner."

"Will you take me to Maria's?" asked Francesa.

"Yes. Yes. I will take you to Maria's."

"Then I will give you thirty minutes."

For the moment Francesca was happy. Unfortunately, it never lasted long. Soon she would demand they go for dessert, or shopping, or to some social engagement with her friends. It was always about what she wanted – in fact, demanded. And it was all very one-sided.

"Don't you love me?" He heard Francesca's voice in his head. *"Yes, I love you,"* he had replied. He tried to focus on the screen. He clicked on the mouse and advanced through the scene. But a dialogue had begun in his head. He pictured himself in conversation with Francesca.

"Yes, I love you. I just don't think that I can marry you." Yeah, right, he thought to himself. *Like I could ever say that to her.*

Matteo thought about how his family would disown him. The Parisi family would feel dishonored and betrayed. And what about Francesca? She would be embarrassed and devastated. No. It is easier to just keep things as they are.

He figured that he would start his film career, then marry Francesca. Everyone will live happily ever after. *Or, in my case*, he thought, *content ever after. But you can do a lot worse than being content*, he reasoned. Matteo rubbed his eyes and went back to editing. *At least you can control the outcome of this film*, he thought.

CHAPTER 3

Amanda

The text message was from my sister, Holly. Normally I would love to hear from her. Or my brother Scott, or my parents. But, lately, it seems that all of our conversations revolve around the family drama with my sister Tina.

Scott is the eldest child. He is two years older than me and an Economics professor at Boston College. Holly is two years younger than I am. She is a Kindergarten teacher in a suburb of Boston. Tina is the youngest. She is four years younger than me. She barely graduated from college a year ago and has only spiraled downward since.

I love Tina, as I do all my siblings, but she is far from my favorite. She has a need to create constant drama in her life. If something isn't wrong with her life, she creates a problem. Then she either looks for sympathy or complains about how "everything bad happens to her."

I know that stuff happens. I also know some folks seem to have more to deal with than others. I get that. I really do. But that's not Tina. No. Tina invites or invents all of her troubles. Then she drags the rest of the family into the middle of whatever she has manufactured.

I read Holly's text.

Holly: You won't believe the latest from Tina. She managed to get herself fired from another job, evicted from her apartment, and her latest boyfriend just got arrested on drug charges. Now she wants us to post the loser's bail and for Mom and Dad to give them both a place to stay.

Me: Like that is going to happen.

Holly: No kidding. You know Mom and Dad will give Tina a place to stay, but not her boyfriend of the week.

Me: Each boyfriend is worse than the last. At least if Tina is at Mom and Dad's they can keep an eye on her. Not that they should have to. She's 23, for crying out loud.

Holly: Exactly. My lunch break is almost over, but I wanted to give you a heads up. Tina's already hit up Scott and me for cash. Two strikes, so you're up.

Me: Thanks for the warning. Let's talk later. Tina really needs help. Maybe some sort of intervention.

Holly: Agreed. She needs to realize that she isn't a victim. She brings all this stuff on herself.

Me: Talk later. Luv ya, bye.

Holly. Later. Bye. Luv ya, too.

Each episode with Tina has more elements of drama than the one before. We've tried everything we can think of to help her. She just claims she's a victim of bad luck rather than bad decisions. Frankly, we were now at a loss as to what to do to help her. We've tried counseling, heart-to-heart talks, everything we can think of.

One thing we did know, giving bail money for her druggie boyfriend wasn't going to help anyone. Whoever he was, he needed to be in rehab. I knew that my dad would help find the guy a program, but Tina needed to stay away from him. The last thing we needed was for her to get on drugs too. Her life was messed up enough.

I knew that I would need to talk to Tina at some point. But I didn't want to deal with her attitude when I tell her I wouldn't be giving her bail money. I also wanted to figure out what I might say to her. I needed some good options for helping her. I didn't have any at the moment. I'd exhausted all my good ideas months ago.

For now, I turned off my phone. I picked up the first student paper in the pile and began reading. I made it about a third of the way through the paper. But I felt a little guilty. I knew that Tina had probably tried calling by now. She's a mess and a pain in the butt. She has refused any real help numerous times. But she is my sister.

"Darn it!" I said out loud.

I put down the paper and picked up my phone. I turned it on and waited for the alert that I had a new voice mail message. Sure enough. I listened. Tina was all sunshine and roses. Sadly, I knew it was a ploy to bait me into calling. She wanted me to walk right into her sob story to hit me up for the money. I took the bait.

Guilt can be a real nuisance. Especially when you have no reason to feel guilty. But you do all the same. I scrolled through my contacts and dialed Tina's number.

"Hi big sister," she said as she answered the phone. She was little miss sunshine. I gave her about thirty seconds before she laid into me with her story.

"Hey, Tina. I saw that you called. I'm in the middle of grading papers, so I only have a few minutes. What's up?"

"Of course you only have a few minutes. Scott, Holly, and you are always busy doing something. Nobody ever has any time for their little sister."

"Tina, that's not true. But on a weekday during the school year, yes, we are busy. We have work to do."

"Oh right! My perfect brother and sisters. You all have jobs. I forgot. I'm the loser who no one will give a job to."

"Holly, you are not a loser. And plenty of people have given you jobs."

"So, what? Are you saying I can't keep a job? Is that it? You don't know anything about how hard things are for me. I have the worst luck. I always end up in a crappy situation at work. Somebody is always out to get me. To get me fired."

"Tina, do you seriously think that is the case at every job you have ever had?"

"You weren't at those jobs. You don't know."

"Tina, is there something you want? I really need to get these papers graded before my class."

"Ricky, you know, my boyfriend?"

"No, I don't. The last time I talked to you, three weeks ago, you were dating a guy named Steve."

"Steve's history."

"Lovely," I said.

"I met Ricky in a bar last week."

"Uh huh."

"Well, a friend of Ricky's hid some drugs in Ricky's car. Ricky got pulled over and the cops found the drugs."

"Tina, were they Ricky's drugs? Be honest."

"No. They weren't. Not this time."

"Not this time? There are other times where the drugs were his?"

"Ricky just does a little weed. It helps relax him."

"What did he get pulled over for?"

"Ricky?"

"Yes. Ricky."

"DUI."

"Tina, anyway you slice this, Ricky probably needs a night or two in jail and then he needs to get himself into rehab."

"How did you know he was in jail?"

"Lucky guess."

"Did Holly or Steve call you?"

"That's irrelevant," I replied.

"I bet Holly called you. The two of you are always ganging up on me."

"Hey! Not true."

"Little Miss Perfect. Oh, I forgot, that is you," said Tina.

"I've heard more than enough and your two minutes were up five minutes ago."

"Amanda, wait!"

"What?"

"I really need some money. Enough to get Ricky out of jail so we can get him into a rehab program. You know, like you said."

"Does Ricky want to go to rehab?"

It was a foolish question. I already knew the answer. There was silence on the other end of the phone.

"Tina?" I said after a few beats of silence.

"Yeah?"

"Does Ricky want to go to rehab?"

"No. But he'll go if I ask him to."

"Because you have so much invested in your relationship?"

"That's not fair," said Tina.

"You have only been dating him a week. You probably barely know the guy. At least I hope you don't know him very well. I'd hate to think you knowingly started dating a drug addict."

"He sells more than he uses."

"Tina, you need to stop talking. Your plea for Ricky's bail is getting worse by the second."

"So you're not going to send me the money?"

"What do you think? Tina, please go stay with Mom and Dad. At least for a little while. We'll all talk soon and figure things out. But right now, you need to forget about Ricky. Trust me, there is no future with him."

"Thanks for nothing!" Tina said. Then she ended our call.

I called my dad and made sure he knew to go find Tina and bring her home. He told me that Scott had already called. Plus the landlord who was evicting Tina. My parents had to co-sign just for her to get the place. My dad was in the car on his way to Tina's. He was going to settle her last month's rent and then take her back to my parents.

I looked at the time. Three hours before my class. I don't know why I thought I would have time for lunch with Brad. Tina's latest drama didn't help. I sent Brad a text. He would understand and we would try tomorrow.

It would take a small miracle to get all the papers finished in time, but I was going to give it my best. I would, however, need a third cup of coffee.

CHAPTER 4

I managed to get all the papers graded in time. After class I made my way to the graduate teaching office in my department. Each graduate student who taught undergraduate courses had a desk in the office. Heather Banks and Allen Chandler were at their desks when I arrived.

Heather was finishing her third year in the doctoral program. Allen was in his fourth. That meant that we were four years into his asking me out and my saying no. Allen was a nice enough guy, but I had zero interest in dating him. We weren't even close friends. He looked up from his desk as soon as I walked in.

"Hi, Amanda," he greeted me.

"Hi, Allen. Hi, Heather," I said.

Heather was on the phone. She smiled and waved.

"So, I see you have your dissertation defense scheduled for next Wednesday," Allen said to me.

"Yep," I replied. I found that short answers worked best with Allen. My philosophy had been to minimize my time of engagement with him. He had in his mind that I was just playing hard to get. I didn't see any reason to provide false encouragement that I was actually interested in him.

"Unfortunately, I am teaching a class at that time," Allen said.

"Too bad."

"Maybe I can get a teaching assistant to cover for me. The topic of your thesis fascinates me."

"U huh," I replied as I flipped through the mail on my desk. I didn't want to be rude, but Allen never took a hint. Heck, he didn't take my directly telling him I had no interest, and I was dating someone. He just kept at it, no matter what.

"How are your interviews going? You know, for full-time teaching positions?"

"Fine. Thank you."

"I hear that you are a finalist for an Assistant Professor position in the UCLA Classics department."

"Yes. That is common knowledge in the department."

Another tactic I had recently taken with Allen was to make him aware that everything he knew about me was public information. At least public within the Classics department at USC. Therefore, he was not part of my inner circle. He didn't know anything personal about me. I'm not sure it registered with him.

"I bet you get the position. You would be great at UCLA. Plus it has the added benefit that you would still be in LA."

I put the stack of mail down and looked at Allen. "And, exactly, why is that a benefit?"

He paused a few beats. Ah ha! I may finally have stumped him.

"You know, close to all your friends here at USC," he finally replied.

"I guess there is that, Allen. Excuse me, I have a note to go see Professor Lane." I flashed the pink memo sheet for added credibility. I stepped around Allen and headed toward the office door.

"Ah, okay. Catch you later," Allen called after me.

The memo actually was about seeing Professor Lane. Robert Lane was my academic adviser and mentor. He had been a professor at USC for fifteen years and is a leading scholar in our field. It was on his recommendation that I was a candidate for the position at UCLA.

I walked down the hall and knocked on his office door.

"Come in," I heard him call from inside his office.

I opened the door and entered. "You wanted to see me?" I said.

"Amanda, hello. Yes. Please come in and have a seat."

Professor Lane cleared a stack of books off the chair next to his desk. His tiny office was filled with books. Stacks and stacks of books. He long had run out of space on the bookcase that took up an entire wall. Now books were stacked where ever he had an empty spot. He held the books in his arms and looked around for a spot to place them.

"Here we go," he said when he located a clearing on his windowsill. He put the books down and turned back around toward me.

"How was your class this afternoon?" he asked me.

"Fine. They are all very good students. Their papers were exceptional. I expect good results from them on the final exam."

"Excellent. Now, speaking of exams . . . how are you feeling about your oral defense?"

"I feel fine," I said with a faint smile. "Just as I have the last hundred times you have asked me this week."

He was my faculty adviser, and I had taken all of his courses, but in the past few years we had become more like friends. He was a sweet man and had a brilliant mind. It was also no secret I was his favorite student.

Professor Lane chuckled warmly. "I guess I have asked you quite a bit, haven't I?"

"I think you are more nervous about my dissertation defense than I am."

"You are probably correct. I just want everything to go perfectly for you."

"I'm sure it will be fine. My research is solid. You told me so yourself."

"True. True," he replied. "I really have no concerns about your work."

"Then why are you so nervous?" I asked.

"Amanda, it is no secret how fond I am of you. I guess I am nervous like a parent would be. This is such a big moment. I have it on good authority that all you need to do is have your doctorate in hand and the assistant professor position at UCLA is yours."

"Should you be telling me that?"

"Probably not," he said with a wry smile. "But it is very likely that at least a few of the faculty from their department will attend your defense. You know, to see you in action."

"Okay. Now I am little nervous."

"I'm sorry. That was not my intent. I just didn't want you to walk in that room next week and be surprised. I figured that it is better for you to know. It doesn't change a thing about your research or the questions that are likely to be asked by the dissertation committee. Or, for that matter, how you will answer."

"You just didn't want me to get distracted and tripped up by the UCLA faculty being present," I said.

"Exactly. If you know in advance that they will be there, you will expect it and can put it out of your mind."

"Except that I could mess up and not only not get my PhD, but I could lose the best chance that I have at a full-time teaching position."

"Amanda, dear, do you honestly think that is what is going to happen?"

I paused a beat.

"No. I guess not."

"Me either. I don't want you to get all cocky, but you are going to ace this just as you have everything else since you started this program five years ago. Actually, since you started here as an undergraduate student. This is but the last step of many that you have excelled at along the way."

"Thank you," I said.

"You're welcome. Now, do you have time to join me for lunch tomorrow? There is something else that I would like to discuss with you."

"Sure. Lunch tomorrow would be great. Is anything wrong?"

"Not at all. But you have to wait until tomorrow. How about Noon at the University Club?"

"Okay. Sounds wonderful."

"Excellent. I have a faculty meeting tomorrow morning. Why don't I meet you there at Noon."

"Noon it is. See you then."

As I left Professor Lane's office, my cell phone rang. Lately, with all the drama with Tina, I dreaded having to check my phone. Fortunately, it was my best friend, Jenny. We had attended USC together as undergraduates. Since then Jenny has worked in the marketing department at Pacific Coast Pictures.

"Hi, Jenny," I answered.

"Okay, tell me you are not nervous about your dissertation defense next week," Jenny said.

"I haven't been," I said, "but you, my family, and Professor Lane are going to make me nervous if you all keep asking me if I am nervous."

"I didn't ask if you were nervous. I wanted you to tell me that you are not nervous. Because you shouldn't be."

I tried to wrap my head around Jenny's statement.

"I think that is kind of the same thing as asking me if I'm nervous."

"There is nothing for you to be nervous about. I just wanted to check in."

"I'm fine," I said.

"Any more drama with Tina?"

"I'll fill you in later. On the upside, I think I am going to be offered the position at UCLA."

"That is awesome! I am really hoping you can stay in Los Angeles. What would I do without my best friend living nearby?"

"Same thing I would do . . . be sad and spend a lot of time Skyping."

"I gotta go," said Jenny, "I have a department meeting starting in a few minutes. We still on for tonight?"

"Absolutely. Seven o'clock?"

"Sounds good. Later."

"Bye."

Jenny and I were getting together for our weekly girls night out. My schedule was crazy, but I made sure to always have that evening each week with Jenny. I honestly couldn't imagine my life without her. I was as close to Jenny as I was with Holly. Maybe even closer. I was definitely closer to Jenny than I was with Tina. Although that wouldn't take much.

I stepped out into the California sunshine. A warm breeze was blowing across campus. Despite those days when the LA smog was as thick as pea soup, I loved the southern California weather. *Here's to staying in Los Angeles*, I thought as I crossed the quad.

CHAPTER 5

At Noon the following day I waited outside the USC University Club. It was a club for faculty, staff, and their invited guests. I had been Professor Lane's invited guest several times over the course of my graduate studies. I liked the food in the restaurant. It was a treat for a student to eat at the club.

At 12:05 PM, Professor Lane hurried to where I was waiting.

"I am sorry that I am late. Professor Rubens would not stop talking at the faculty meeting," he said as he approached me.

"Not a problem," I replied. I giggled. "I remember Professor Rubens being like that in class as well."

"Yes. Well, Gerald never met a word in the English language that he did not like. The same holds true for Latin and Greek. Come, let's eat."

It was a beautiful day, most are in Southern California, so we decided to sit on the patio. A moment later the waitress came over.

"Good afternoon, Professor Lane. How are you today?" she said.

"I'm doing well, Lucy. How are you?"

"Hanging in there," Lucy replied.

"Lucy, this is one of my finest graduate students, Amanda Evans. She defends her dissertation next week."

"Nice to me and congratulations," Lucy said to me.

"Thank you," I replied.

"Can I get you something to drink?" Lucy asked us.

"water with lemon, please," I said.

"Diet Coke for me," said Professor Lane.

"I'll be right back," said Lucy.

"What looks good to you?" asked Professor Lane as we looked over our menus.

"Everything," I replied.

"Order whatever you want. It is my treat."

A few minutes later Lucy returned with our drinks.

"Are you ready to order or do you need some more time?" Lucy asked.

"Amanda?" said Professor Lane.

"I'm ready if you are," I said.

"Go right ahead," he replied.

"I'll have a cup of Tortilla Soup and the Cobb Salad," I said.

"And for you, Professor?" asked Lucy.

"I will have the soup of the day and the Tuscan Grilled Chicken Sandwich."

"Thank you," Lucy said as we handed her our menus.

"I'm not going to ask you if you are nervous about your dissertation defense," Professor Lane announced.

"That's a relief," I replied.

"I do, however, want to know if you would be interested in teaching a summer course in Rome?"

"Me? Teach a summer course in Rome?"

"Yes. We have a group of undergraduates participating in the American Academy in Rome Classical Summer School. They have an excellent faculty, but they have asked us if we would be willing to have one of our faculty teach a course."

"But I am not a USC faculty member."

"You are an Instructor for introductory undergraduate Classics courses. You are a week away from earning your doctorate. You will be an Assistant Professor of Classical Studies at UCLA next fall. You are qualified."

"I appreciate your confidence in me. However, I have yet to pass my oral defense. Nor have I received an actual job offer from UCLA."

"All formalities at this point," said Professor Lane with a wave of his hand.

Lucy came with our soups.

"Your main course should be out shortly," she announced as she placed our soups on the table. "Anything else that I can get for you?"

We told her that we were good.

"Enjoy the soup." She retreated with a warm smile.

"So what do you think about the summer program?" asked Professor Lane.

"I am very interested. But this is rather last minute. Was this an unexpected request from the Academy? Are there no faculty, full-time professors, I mean, who want to teach the course?"

"I was scheduled to teach the course myself, but something has come up and I will not be able to go to Rome this summer. I could ask another faculty member to go in my place, but they have all had some experience teaching in either Rome or Athens. I thought that this would be a good opportunity for you. Another feather in your cap, so to speak."

"And the Academy in Rome is okay with the idea of my teaching the course instead of you?"

"Yes. I have already spoken to them. I assured them of your qualifications. I told them that I hand picked you to teach the course in my place."

"Well, I am honored. When is the program?"

"The first two weeks in July."

"Wow. That is only six weeks away."

"Yes. But your passport is current?"

"Yes."

"You know the material like the back of your hand. You graduate in three weeks. It would give you three full weeks to prepare. And all we need to do is make the change on the flight and room reservations. Everything is included."

"Okay. I'll do it. Thank you so much for asking me."

"You are most welcome. I am delighted that you have agreed. If you can, you should extend your time in Italy. Add a vacation onto the end of the trip. Just let me know so we can extend the return date for the flight."

"That sounds like a great idea. My family has been asking me what I want as a gift for earning my PhD. I think them contributing toward a week or two in Italy would do nicely."

"Wonderful. By the way, will your entire family be coming out for graduation?"

"Yes. Well, most of them will be. My parents, my brother Scott, and my sister Holly."

"You have a second sister? She not able to make it?"

"I highly doubt it. That is a long story."

"No need to say any more," said Professor Lane. "I understand all about family drama."

Professor Lane didn't offer anything more and, naturally, I didn't ask. I did, however, wonder if it had anything to do with his not being able to go to Rome. Or, it could have been a general statement. Most families have at least a little drama and dysfunction in their history.

Our lunch came, and we enjoyed more casual conversation as we ate. After lunch we said our goodbyes.

"Don't forget," said Professor Lane, "let me know if you want to extend your time in Italy so we can change the return flight."

"I will talk to my family and let you know by the end of the week."

Professor Lane gave me a nod of the head and a wave of the hand with a warm smile. Then he turned and headed toward the parking lot. I couldn't believe it. I was going to be teaching a summer course in Rome. Professor Lane was right, this was a good opportunity for me. What neither of us knew was how much this trip would change my life.

CHAPTER 6

I met Jenny later that evening at the Pizza Studio near the USC campus.

"I haven't eaten here before," said Jenny. "It looks cool."

"It's great," I replied. "You get to build your own pizza. You select the crust, sauce, and toppings."

"Ah," said Jenny. "Hence the name *Pizza Studio*."

"Exactly. So what should we order?"

"I don't know. What are you thinking?"

"I'm between the Whole grain and flax seed or Rosemary Herb for the crust. I like to go traditional for the sauce and then a blend of fresh mozzarella and feta cheeses. And I'm open to almost any toppings," I said.

"How about the Rosemary Herb crust, the traditional sauce, mozzarella and feta cheeses, and then green bell peppers and caramelized onions for the toppings?" said Jenny.

"Perfect," I said.

We ordered our pizza and then found a table.

"I have lots to catch you up on, but I first want to hear how your date with Jeremy went," I said as soon as we sat down.

"What can I say about my date with Jeremy Wagner? . . . Only that we had the most incredible time."

"I am so happy it went well," I said. "He took so long to ask you out. I'm glad it was worth the wait."

"It was definitely worth the wait," Jenny replied.

We both squealed like little girls. The excitement of the moment got the best of both of us. We attracted some glances our way, but the other patrons quickly went back to eating pizza and their own conversations.

"We have been friends for quite some time," Jenny said. "We work closely on projects in the office, we have spent considerable time together at social events outside of work, and there has always been a chemistry between us."

"So why did he take so long to ask you out?"

"He got really hung up on an old flame from high school. Somebody named Ashley. She was all he talked about for a while. It was really annoying. Apparently they bumped into each other when he was visiting a friend in New York. Then it looked like she was going to take a job here in LA."

"So what happened?"

"She ended up getting back together with the guy she had been dating. You'll never guess who that was."

"Who?" I asked.

"Brandon Mitchell."

"The cute CEO of Davenport Media? The one who used to be in all the magazines?"

"One and the same."

"Don't read as much about him anymore."

"I guess he's domesticated now. I read he and Ashley got married."

"And Jeremy was really hung up on this Ashley?"

"I think he had carried a torch for her since high school. Don't get me wrong, he didn't obsess over her or anything. In fact, I doubt he even gave her much of a second thought until he ran into her in New York. I mean he dated regularly and I never heard him mention her until after his trip to New York. I don't know, I guess seeing her again, under the right circumstances, reignited a bit of the flame. But after she got back together with Brandon Mitchell that was that."

"Okay, so what changed between the two of you?" I asked.

"I think one of his buddies in the office gave him a kick in the butt and told him that what he wanted had been in front of him all along. Apparently he agreed and asked me out."

"When are you going out with him again?"

"Friday night. We're going to a Dodgers game."

"You don't like baseball."

"But Jeremy does. He's a rabid Dodgers fan."

"I can't wait to meet him," I said.

"We should set up a double date," offered Jenny.

I paused a beat too long.

"What's wrong?" asked Jenny.

"Nothing's wrong. I just think that Brad and I have reached the end of our time together. Graduation is in a few weeks and then he leaves to work with some wide receiver coach before he reports to training camp."

"How do you feel about that?" asked Jenny. "I know you two never had any plans of staying together, but Brad is a really nice guy. Very cute, too."

"Yes, he is both of those things. But, you're right, we have never had any intention of staying together beyond graduation. That hasn't changed. I'm a little sad it will be over, but he's not the one for me and I'm not the one for him. We never were. We've always known that. But we were good together for what it was."

"And you were clear on what it wasn't?"

"Exactly. So I am okay with it. We both are. Besides, I will have so much going on, I won't have any time to think about a man for a while," I said.

"There is always time to think about a man."

"I guess that's true. But let's just say I will have a lot of other things going on and it won't be foremost in my mind for a while."

"Okay. Fair enough," Jenny agreed with a smile. "So, tell me what is going on."

"I will be spending July in Italy."

"Italy? That sounds exciting."

"Professor Lane asked me to fill in for the classical summer program at the American Academy in Rome. It is a two week course and then I am going to stay for two weeks of vacation."

"That sounds like so much fun. I'm jealous."

"You should come for the second two weeks in July. We can vacation together.," I said.

"I'd love to. And believe me, I though of it as soon as you told me, but we have one of the biggest movie premiers of the year coming up this summer. It's all hands on deck in the marketing department. I probably won't see the California sunshine until August."

"Bummer. I will take lots of pictures. Maybe we can plan a getaway for the winter."

"I can definitely get on board with that."

Our pizza arrived. It smelled so wonderful. It tasted as good as it smelled.

"I know that I am not supposed to ask," said Jenny, "but how are you feeling about your dissertation defense next week?"

"Fine. I am, surprisingly, very relaxed about it. I don't think I am overconfident, but I've worked hard and Professor Lane is confident in my work. That speaks volumes. There are few in the field of Classics as respected as he is. I did get a little nervous when he told me that some of the UCLA faculty on the hiring committee may attend."

"Really?" asked Jenny. "I thought you said that it looked like you had the job."

"Yes. I think it is one last opportunity to check me out. See me in action as Professor Lane put it. But as I have thought about it, they won't be hearing anything that I haven't already discussed with them. Heck, they have all read my dissertation. If they had any concerns, I wouldn't be this close to being offered the position."

"So it is more of a formality?"

"You could say that. Professor Lane isn't worried, so I'm not going to worry. Besides, that wouldn't change a thing. The only reason he told me they were likely to be there is so I didn't freak out at their presence the day of my defense."

"Time to process the fact that they are coming? No surprises?"

"Exactly. Now I'm not surprised and I am more than okay with them being there."

"Well, I've already taken the morning off, so I will be there with bells on. I won't understand most of it, but you have my full moral support."

"I always do," I replied. "And knowing you will be there really means a lot to me."

"I wouldn't miss it for the world. I want to be the first to call you Doctor Amanda Evans."

"Fingers crossed," I said crossing my fingers.

"You've got this," said Jenny warmly.

As we finished our pizza, we talked more about my plans for Italy, Jenny's projects at work, and general girl stuff. All-in-all, a fun evening with my BFF. It was the perfect way to prepare for the mad dash to the finish line of the academic year.

CHAPTER 7

The following week I had a successful oral defense of my dissertation. Jenny wasn't the first to congratulate me and call me "Dr. Evans." Professor Lane beat her to it. As it should be, I guess. Protocol and all. But she was the second. Third in line was the department chair from the UCLA faculty. After offering congratulations, she offered me the position of Assistant Professor. I immediately accepted.

I called my family and gave them the news. I saw them the following week when they came for my graduation. Minus Tina. Not that I was surprised by her absence. At least she was staying with my parents and my dad was able to get her a job at his company. It was a step in the right direction for her.

Brad and I said our goodbyes and parted as good friends. I spent the next three weeks preparing to teach my summer course and planning my vacation. The time sped by and the next thing I knew I was in Rome.

I was excited about the opportunity to teach in the summer program at the Academy. I was taken by the beauty of the property that sat on Janiculum Hill with a sweeping view of Rome. The American Academy in Rome was a hive of activity with the Classical Summer School, the Summer Program in Archaeology, and even a Summer Program in Roman Pottery.

"Good afternoon, Dr. Evans, it is a pleasure to meet you," greeted the head of the Classical Studies program. It took a moment for it to register that he was speaking to me. I still wasn't used to being referred to as "Doctor." I would probably be more comfortable with "Professor" once I started teaching at UCLA. I greeted the director, and he gave me a tour of the school.

"The Classical Studies program was founded in 1895 as the American School of Classical Studies in Rome, which merged into the Academy in 1913," he told me as we walked the grounds. "Classical Studies offers several summer programs in the humanities, so numerous classes will be going on during your time here."

After my tour, I settled into my room in The Villa Aurelia. It was a mansion originally built for Cardinal Girolamo Farnese around 1650. It is the setting for conferences, public receptions, concerts, programs, and includes apartments for the Academy's Residents. I looked out the window of my room at the magnificent gardens that surrounded The Villa Aurelia. I made a mental note to be walk the gardens every chance that I got over the next two weeks. First, however, I wanted to check out the library.

The library was tranquil, silent, and elegant. I was told that it had been redesigned and renovated in 2006/2007. It offered a perfect blend of the past with the technological demands of contemporary research. I read that the library was built above the ancient aqueduct of the emperor Trajan. So much history, just right where I stood.

I looked through the library's treasure trove of invaluable collections in history, archaeology, and the art of Rome and Italy. I spent over an hour looking at the extensive photographic archive documenting Rome's many monuments. I couldn't wait to explore the city as part of the summer course. But that wouldn't allow me all the time that I wanted to see everything, so I was glad that I had two additional weeks to take in the city on my own. But all of that would have to wait, I had a class to teach.

CHAPTER 8

The first two weeks of July went by quickly. To say that I enjoyed teaching as part of the Classics Summer Program would be an understatement. I had an amazing time. The nerdy professor in me soaked up every moment of it. But I was also looking forward to my vacation. But before I left the Academy for my hotel, I wanted to take another walk through my favorite parts of the gardens.

There were eleven acres of organically cultivated gardens atop the Janiculum Hill, an area in Rome with a long history of gardens. A guide for the gardens had told a small group of us earlier in the week that the gardens were home to twelve varieties of butterflies and were a haven for hedgehogs, robins, herons, blue tits, woodpeckers, lizards, and a variety of bees.

I smiled as I remembered that a tween boy had nudged his friend and giggled. "That lady said 'tits'," he had remarked. They both got a good laugh out of it. I never understood that boyhood humor, but I remembered that my brother was just like that at their age. I guessed it was normal.

I finished walking the gardens and headed back to collect my luggage from my room in The Villa Aurelia. As I rounded the corner I nearly walked directly into the most handsome young man that I had ever laid eyes on. To be more accurate, he nearly walked directly into me.

"Mi scusi," he said to me. He was clearly embarrassed at nearly running into me.

"Nessun problema," I replied.

"Your Italian is perfect. But your accent . . . you are American?"

"Your English is equally perfect, but you are Italian?" I said playfully.

I guess I was trying to flirt. At least sound witty. I honestly couldn't think clearly. With just a few words he drew me in. And it was more than his Italian accent. It was more than how gorgeous he was. He had an aura about him the took my breath away.

I found myself gazing at him. It was as if the world around us stopped for a moment and it was just the two of us. I took in every inch of his tall, thin frame.

He had wavy black hair, piercing dark eyes, and flawless olive skin. A few strands of his hair hung in a curl on his forehead. His sideburns met the upper parts of the five o'clock shadow on his face. He had a warm smile and delectably full lips.

His laugh broke my momentary trance.

"Yes," he replied. "But I am afraid that I was living, how do you say it, too much inside of my head. I was not paying enough attention to my surroundings. Or, perhaps too much, and not watching where I was going."

"Well, it is very easy to get caught up in the beauty that surrounds us," I replied.

"Indeed," he said softly as he looked into my eyes. "Dove sono i miei modi? . . .Where are my manners? I am Matteo Rosetti." He held out his hand.

"Amanda Evans. It is a pleasure to meet you." When he touched my hand, my heart skipped a beat. A warmth radiated throughout my body.

"Are you a teacher or student here?" Matteo asked me.

"I just finished teaching a two week summer course in the Classics."

"Ah. So you are a professor?"

"Sort of," I said.

Matteo wrinkled his nose and titled his head. It was adorable. Like a little puppy. But not like a puppy because Matteo was smoldering hot. I was about to burn up just standing in front of him.

"I mean yes. I mean . . . I just earned my doctorate and I will begin teaching as an assistant professor in the fall."

"Congratulations, Professor Evans. Will you be teaching here?"

"Thank you. Oh, no. I will be teaching at UCLA – the University of California in Los Angeles."

"Los Angeles!" Matteo said as his eyes lit up like a Christmas tree. "Hollywood!"

"Yes," I said with a slight giggle. "Do you like Hollywood movies?"

"I love all cinema. I am a filmmaker. It is my dream to direct movies in Hollywood one day."

Andre, a staff member from The Villa Aurelia approached.

"Excuse me," Andre said. "Pardon my interrupting. Dr. Evans, your taxi has arrived to take you to your hotel."

"Oh, yes. Thank you," I said. "I was just on my way to get my luggage."

"If you like, I can send someone to your room to retrieve your luggage," offered Andre.

"Yes. That would be nice. Thank you, Andre."

"You are most welcome, Dr. Evans. I hope you enjoyed your stay with us and that the summer program was a success."

"I very much enjoyed my stay. And, yes, the program went very well. Thank you."

"I hope that we see you again in the future," said Andre.

"Thank you. I hope so as well."

"I will let the taxi driver know that you will be out in a few minutes."

"Thank you, Andre."

Andre turned and left.

"I am sorry, it seems that I am interrupting your day," said Matteo.

"Oh, no. Not at all. To be honest, I was enjoying talking to you so much that I forgot that the taxi was coming for me."

"Ah. See, it is my fault."

"You are only guilty of being nice," I replied with the flirtiest smile I could muster.

"I do not mean to pry into your business, but the gentleman stated that you are going to a hotel. Are you staying longer in Rome?"

"You are not prying. Yes. I am spending two weeks in Rome for vacation."

"I don't want to seem forward, but I would be very happy to show you some of the sites one day during your visit. Although, being a Classics professor, you probably know more than I do about the city."

"Oh, I wouldn't be so sure. I have knowledge from books. You have knowledge from experience. From living in the city. You understand the culture in a way that I do not."

"Is that a 'yes'?"

"Oh. Yes. I would love to see some of the sights with you."

"Excellent. Let me give you my number."

"Here," I said as I handed Matteo my cell phone. "Why don't you input your number and I'll do the same with your phone."

"See, that is why you have a PhD," he said with a smile.

He took my phone and handed me his. We entered our numbers and then handed our phones back to each other.

"We can talk about movies, too," I said, "I am a bit of a movie buff."

"Wonderful. I was hoping that you could tell me a little about Hollywood."

"I don't know that much, but I have been on studio tours. Oh, and my best friend works in the marketing department of one of the studios. She knows a ton about how the movie business works."

Matteo's eyes got even wider with excitement. "I have to meet the editor of my current project, but I am free all tomorrow afternoon. Can I call you later tomorrow morning? Perhaps we could meet for lunch and then spend the afternoon touring the city?"

"That sounds perfect," I said. "See you tomorrow."

"Addio, mia bella nuovo amico. Ci vediamo domani (*Goodbye, my lovely new friend. See you tomorrow),* said Matteo.

I smiled and gave a wave as I turned toward the front entrance. I didn't even care about the meter running on the waiting taxi. Whatever the cost, it was worth it. I felt like a school girl who had just been asked on a date by the cutest boy in school.

CHAPTER 9

"Do you think love at first sight is possible?" I asked Jenny over the phone as I sat in the cafe of my hotel.

"I guess anything is possible," she replied. "Why? Have you met some handsome Italian guy?" she said jokingly.

"Actually, I have."

"What?! And you think you are in love?! Amanda, get a grip. I think you are spending too much time in the July heat."

"I didn't say I was in love. I just said that I did meet a handsome Italian guy."

"But you prefaced it by asking if I thought love at first sight was possible."

"True. But I am not saying that is what is going on here. I will say, however, I felt this instant connection to Matteo. That's his name. I could hardly believe it. I mean, the only thing I know about him is that he is a film student here in Rome."

"Well then, by all means, lets get you measured for a wedding gown," said Jenny.

"There is no need to be sarcastic," I said.

"See, this is what happens when you travel by yourself. You may be book smart, but its moments like this that I question your common sense."

"So you are saying that I have had other moments like this?"

"Not just like this, but you get my point."

"No. Actually, I don't," I said.

"Never mind. So What's the deal with this Matteo?"

"I don't know. He is meeting me in a few minutes to show me around Rome this afternoon."

"Are you sure it is a good idea? You don't even know this guy."

"First, we are going to all tourist attractions. It's not like I am going to walk down a deserted, dark alley with him. Second, I met him at the American Academy in Rome. Not some seedy bar. Third . . ., well, third, he is totally adorable. Jenny, you wouldn't believe how handsome he is. And he a definite charm about him. He instantly drew me in."

"Just be careful," Jenny said.

"I will. Oh, here he comes. I'll talk to you later." I ended our call and placed my phone into my backpack.

"Good afternoon, Amanda," greeted Matteo. He kissed my hand. I thought I might melt.

"Good afternoon, Matteo."

He sat opposite me. The waiter came over and handed Matteo a menu and took his drink order. We looked over the menus so we would be ready to order when the waiter came back. We ordered sandwiches for a quick lunch.

"What did you see this morning?" Matteo asked me.

"The Coliseum. You know, I have studied Roman history, language, and culture for years, but being in the Coliseum, it really came alive for me."

"The Coliseum is a must see. So I am glad that you got there already. I was thinking I would take you to Le Domus Romane di Palazzo Valentini. It is amazing. Part of the tour is a multimedia gallery that takes you back to what Rome was like 2,000 years ago. It is very well done. You will not be disappointed. I promise."

"Okay. I am sold. How did your meeting with your editor go this morning? What is your film about?"

"It went very well. I am working on a small budget independent film. It is an espionage or thriller about a spy. Sort of the Italian James Bond. That is why I was at The Villa Aurelia at the Academy yesterday. We will be filming a scene there the end of next week."

"So you don't film every day?"

"When I said it was a low-budget independent film, I should have said that it is very low-budget independent film that we work on when we have enough money. We had enough to last us through the end of last week and we are receiving a grant to finish the project next week."

"That must be very frustrating. The financial aspect of it, I mean."

"Yes. It can be. But I wouldn't want to do anything else."

"Where did you go to school to become a filmmaker?"

"I just completed my master's in film study at Centro Sperimentale di Cinematografia – the Experimental Cinema Center. It is Italy's national film school."

"Congratulations," I said.

"Thank you. I am very excited about my final film project. I have entered it in the Student Film Awards and into a contest from one of the Hollywood studios. The winner of the contest gets an internship at the studio as well as a scholarship to post-graduate workshops at the USC School of Cinematic Arts."

"That is very exciting. USC is where I went to school. For both my undergraduate and graduate studies."

"Really? What is USC like? I would love to take classes in their program."

I told Matteo about life at USC and in Los Angeles. I told him all I could remember about the movie studio tours that I had been on. I also shared what I knew about Jenny's work on the marketing side of the movie industry. We had a wonderful lunch that was a mix of talk about movies and Roman culture.

I had the easiest time talking to Matteo. He seemed very comfortable with me as well. We were definitely hitting it off. And I could not deny how attracted I was to him. I wondered if he had a girlfriend. He hadn't mentioned one.

I could listen to Matteo speak all day. Even though he was speaking in perfect English, his accent had the same melodious characteristics as the Italian language itself. He was also the epitome of the beautiful Italian nature. A definite romantic quality. Which made sense. The word "romance" originally meant *from or about Rome*. Being with Matteo, you could feel it.

We finished our lunch and headed toward Le Domus Romane di Palazzo Valentini, which was only a few blocks away. I was familiar with it as the seat of the Province of Rome and much of its history. Nonetheless, I did the tourist thing and picked up a brochure and read:

Palazzo Valentini, seat of the Province of Rome since 1873, was commissioned to be built in 1585 by Cardinal Michele Bonelli, a nephew of Pope Pius V. In the seventeenth century it underwent renovation and a series of extensions were added by Cardinal Carlo Bonelli and Michele Ferdinando Bonelli. The building was partially demolished and then rebuilt by Francesco Peparelli for the new owner, Cardinal Renato Imperiali, who but up an important family library (the 'Imperiali' library), comprising about 24,000 volumes. In the early eighteenth century, the building was leased to several prominent figures, including the Marquis Francesco Maria Ruspoli, who lived there between 1705 and 1713, using it as a private theater and offering hospitality to famous musicians of the time, including George Friedrich Handel, Alessandro Scarlatti and Arcangelo Corelli. The entire building was then purchased in 1752 by Cardinal Giuseppe Spinelli, who moved the Imperial Library to the ground floor for public use and was often frequented by Johann Joachim Winckelmann. In 1827 the Prussian banker and Consul-General Vincenzo Valentini bought the building, making it his home and giving it its name.

"Wait until you see the ruins and the multimedia tour. Very impressive," said Matteo.

It was our groups turn for the tour, so we moved forward and into the building. The building itself was wonderful. But going below the building to the remains of ancient Roman houses uncovered beneath Palazzo Valentini was nothing short of incredible.

"This significantly adds to Rome's already rich historical and artistic heritage," I said to Matteo as we explored the ruins. "This discovery reveals an area that was of great importance in Roman times. It can also help piece together the ancient, medieval and modern topography of Rome. Absolutely fascinating."

Okay, I was getting my geek on. But, hey, I am a Classics professor. I have devoted my adult life to researching, writing about, and teaching this stuff. And now, here I was, standing in ancient Roman ruins. Matteo had a huge smile on his face. He was enjoying the fact that I was having such a good time. How could I not?

I was viewing the fascinating remains of imperial Rome, belonging to powerful families, with mosaics, wall decorations, poly chrome floors, paving blocks, and other remains. I was beside myself.

As we passed into some of the darker rooms I instinctively held out my hand. I had a real fear of the dark as a child. I slept with a night light until I was sixteen. I'm still not crazy about dark spaces. Just as instinctively, Matteo reached out his hand and held mine.

As he wrapped his warm and firm fingers around mine, my knees went weak. His fingers looped through my own made me feel safe.

The multimedia presentation brilliantly recreated the past with virtual reconstructions, graphics and videos. Walls, rooms, kitchens, baths, furnishings and decorations all came to virtual life.

"I was amazed at how the ancient archaeological ruins came together with the modern multimedia presentation to offer a whole new perspective," I said after we finished the tour. "As a filmmaker, the technical and artistic aspects of the video must be especially interesting."

"Yes. They are. I remember when they were working on the multimedia project. Many filmmakers were skeptical. Even cynical. They thought it would be some, how do you say it? . . . cheesy film. Maybe even a bit lame. But what they did is rather brilliant. Now we ask, exactly how did they do that so well?"

"Thank you so much for taking me here. It was amazing," I said.

"I knew you would enjoy it. You were like a little girl unwrapping the present that you most wanted for your birthday. I enjoyed you enjoying the tour."

"You are very sweet."

My phone starting buzzing in my backpack. When I went to reach for my bag, I realized that Matteo and I were still holding hands. I smiled to myself. Our holding hands felt so natural, I guess we both just went with it.

"It's my best friend, Jenny," I said as I looked at my screen. "I'm sorry, just give me a second. Otherwise, Jenny will worry until I call her back."

"No, no. I understand. Please, take your time."

"Hey, Jenny," I answered. I listened for a moment. "No, I am having a great time."

She could tell from the tone in my voice that I was telling the truth. She didn't ask any further questions. I'm sure she figured that I was still with Matteo. She would be dying to know how my day went.

"Okay, I'll talk to you later. Bye," I said. We ended our call, and I tossed my phone back into my bag.

"Your friend, Jenny, she worries about you?"

"Constantly. But she is a wonderful friend."

"It is good to have wonderful friends who care about you," said Matteo.

"It is. You can never have enough."

"I agree," he said with a genuinely warm smile.

CHAPTER 10

Matteo

Matteo woke early the next morning with a smile on his face. He was thinking about Amanda Evans. She was amazing. They had really hit it off. There was a definite connection between them.

Matteo was glad that Francesca hadn't called him last night. The last thing he wanted to do was have a conversation with her. Part of him felt guilty about liking Amanda so much. Part of him wanted to end it with Francesca to be with someone like Amanda. Maybe even Amanda.

But who was he kidding? He knew his future. He was resigned to Francesca being the future Mrs. Matteo Rosetti. While resigned to the fact, he didn't want to think about it.

Matteo made a cup of coffee and sat at the kitchen table. Francesca entered his apartment and padded into the kitchen. So much for not having to speak to Francesca. She sat at the table and took a sip of Matteo's coffee.

"Would you like some?" he asked.

"I have some," she replied with a smirk.

Matteo got up and poured another cup of coffee. He placed it in front of Francesca and then took back the first cup. It was the principle of the thing. Francesca gave him a sideways look. He ignored her.

"All my friends wanted to know where you were last night," she said.

"I had dinner with my family." Which was true. After spending the afternoon with Amanda, Matteo went to his parents for dinner. A weekly ritual.

"Why wasn't I invited?"

"It's an open invitation. You know that. Besides, you had plans with your friends last night."

Francesca shrugged her shoulders and took a sip of her coffee. "You can spend the day with me to make up for excluding me from your family dinner," she said in all seriousness.

"You weren't excluded. Stop playing games."

"Perhaps I can let it slide, for now. I won't be as forgiving when we are married."

Matteo hadn't actually proposed to Francesca, but everyone in the Rosetti and Parisi families knew it was a formality. Matteo decided to sidestep the comment.

"I am meeting a friend," he said after taking a sip of his coffee.

"Who?"

"Pietro. Does it matter?"

"Not really. All your friends are boring."

Matteo let it go. He was tired of arguing with Francesca over everything.

"I'm just saying," she continued, "they are more uptight than my friends. My friends know how to have a good time. Like tomorrow afternoon, we are attending Rome's newest fashion show. It will be sexy."

"The Student Film Awards are tomorrow afternoon. You've known that for two months. It's on the calendar. You know I am nominated for Best Student Film."

Francesca rolled her eyes.

"You know how much I hate those film school events. They are so . . ."

". . . Boring. Yeah, I've heard you tell me that a million times. But I haven't asked you to attend a film school event, any event, actually, in three years. But this is different. I've been nominated for one of the biggest awards. Not that it should matter how big the award is. You should want to be there to support me. In fact, you promised me you would attend."

"I do support you. I hope that you win. And, you're right, I did agree to attend. But it was before I knew about the fashion show. We have VIP passes. I could end up with my picture in the society pages. Or on television."

"You're unbelievable. Do you know that? You don't care about me. All you care about is strutting around so everyone can admire how beautiful you are."

"You think that I am beautiful?"

Francesca stood up and moved toward Matteo and sat on his lap.

"Francesca, get off." Matteo stood abruptly and Francesca backed away.

"What's your problem?!" she screamed. "Is this any way to treat your future wife? Is that the way it is going to be?"

"First, I'm not the one with the problem. You keep saying that you want to be married. But you have no clue about what it means to be in a meaningful relationship. You only care about yourself. Second, I don't remember ever proposing to you. In fact, I have avoided the topic as much as possible."

"Are you saying that you don't want to marry me? I thought we loved each other?"

"Francesca, I'm not saying that we won't get married one day. I don't know. Right now. . . right now, though, you aren't showing me you care at all about what is a huge moment in my life. Because it is important to me, it should matter to you. Whether you think it is boring or not. Whether you care about it or not."

"Fine. I will go to your awards thing."

"No. You have made it very clear you don't want to be there. And it's not just the Student Film Awards. It's . . . it's everything."

"What do you mean?" Francesca asked.

"You really don't get it, do you? . . . I think we need time apart. Some time to think."

"Are you breaking up with me?"

"I'm not saying that. I just want us to have a little space to think about our relationship. Just a few days. Maybe a week. I don't know. Then we can talk."

"I swear Matteo Rosetti, if you leave me it will be the biggest mistake of your pathetic life! Your family will disown you. My family will forget you ever existed. You will be dead to all of us. Cut off."

Matteo nodded his head. He knew she was probably right. It was the only reason he wasn't breaking up with her right then and there. They had a complex relationship that involved not only them, but their families. Pretty much their entire lives.

"I will give you one chance to change your mind," Francesca said as she tapped her foot rapidly.

Matteo looked up and shook his head. "Do you really want to attend the film awards? To be there to support me? Or would you rather go to the fashion show?"

Francesca averted her eyes. "Why do you need to make this hard on me?"

Matteo shook his head. "I think a few days to collect our thoughts is best."

"Fine! Take a few days and think. But we both know how this is going to end up. You belong to me and I am going to be your wife."

There was no easy way out. They both knew it. At least Matteo could get a little breather. Maybe Francesca would miss him and actually think about their relationship. A few days apart could only help the situation. Who was he kidding? Francesca was unlikely to change.

CHAPTER 11

Amanda

Matteo had invited me to attend the Student Film Awards with him. I was excited he asked. I was looking forward to attending with him. It also gave me an excuse to go shopping and buy a new dress. I got a Moschino Black crepe pencil skirt with a hemline above the knee. It was sleeveless with v-neckline wrap detail and an exposed zipper in back. Formal enough for the awards dinner and flirty enough where we could consider this a date.

Matteo arrived at my hotel wearing a slim cut black suit, white shirt, and long black tie. The suit and tie match his dark hair perfectly. The light hint of his cologne was intoxicating.

"Good evening, Amanda. You are absolutely bello. . .beautiful."

"Thank you," I said blushing. "You are very handsome."

"Grazie," he replied.

Matteo held out his arm. I looped my arm through his and he escorted me to his car. He had a two-seat red Fiat sports car. He opened the passenger door for me and I got in. He went around and got in the driver's side.

"This is a cute car," I said.

"A 1980 Fiat Spider," he replied. "It was my father's, and he gave it to me when I graduated high school. She may be over thirty years old, but she runs great."

Matteo started the car, and we were off. It only took us about ten minutes to drive to the film school. The Student Film Awards were being held in a function hall. Tables with fine linens were set up for the dinner. The main stage had a podium and a large banner that read: Premi Cinematografici Studente (Student Film Awards).

"It's not quite the Oscars, but it is a very nice afternoon," said Matteo.

"It looks wonderful. I am so glad that you invited me."

"Yes. Thank you so much for agreeing to attend as my . . . guest."

Guest? I thought to myself. Matteo's English is very good. I was certain he knew the difference between the word "guest" and "date." He had paused a moment. Not sure how to refer to me. We were in an awkward moment. The first since we had met.

"Well, I am honored to be here with you. Delighted, in fact. I really enjoy being with you, and I am so excited about your nomination. This is a big day for you. The fact that you wanted me to be here . . . well, it means a lot. It's special."

Okay, I rambled a bit. I was off my game. The whole "guest" thing had gotten to me. Referring to me as his "date" could still be innocent enough. "Guest" is as platonic as you can get.

"Would you like something to drink?" Matteo asked.

"Yes, please."

We crossed the room to the bar area. We each got a glass of red wine.

"It is an Amarone," said Matteo. "It is a lusty, full-bodied wine from partially dried Corvina grapes, in the Veneto region. It goes very well with flavorful cheeses."

We selected some cheese from the assortment of cheese and crackers and put them on a plate. We enjoyed the wine and cheese and Matteo introduced me to his friends from the film school. Several of them had worked with him on the film that was nominated. They all stayed and chatted for a while and wished Matteo well. Matteo's friend Pietro remained a moment longer.

"If Matteo's film does not win, I will be shocked," said Pietro. "It is, in my opinion, the finest film to be made at the school in years."

"If only Pietro were choosing the winner," said Matteo.

"Did you see Matteo's film?" Pietro asked me.

"I haven't had the opportunity. I'm hoping he shows it to me."

"Well, leave it to Matteo to meet a beautiful woman," said Pietro. "Good luck tonight," he said to Matteo. "I will see you later in the evening. It was nice to meet you, Amanda."

"Nice to meet you as well, Pietro."

"Your friends are very nice," I said.

"Grazie. Yes, we are all very supportive of each other."

"Well, Pietro certainly thinks very highly of your film. I do hope that I will have the opportunity to see it."

"I think I can arrange a showing," said Matteo.

"I look forward to it."

"Amanda, before lunch starts, there is something I have been meaning to discuss with you."

"What's that?"

"Well, I don't know how to say it. You see, it is all very complicated."

"Matteo, I think I know what this is about. You have been very kind. I have enjoyed getting to know you, but we don't need to feel any pressure for this to be one thing or another."

"Amanda, that is just it. I do have feelings about this. I know that we just met, and I don't want to seem forward, but I like you very much. I felt a connection with you from the moment we met. I felt it even more yesterday. I know it may sound crazy . . ."

"No. It is not crazy at all. Or maybe it is. But, then, I am crazy too. I feel a connection as well. I'm just not sure what to do about it."

"For me it is very complicated," said Matteo. "It is why I panicked earlier and referred to you as my guest. Amanda, I have a girlfriend."

"I see. I wish I had known that earlier. Matteo, why am I even the one here with you?"

"You are here with me because you care enough to be here. I have a girlfriend, but I am not happy. We had an argument yesterday morning. I told her I needed some time to think. Amanda, I can't just break up with her. I have known her my entire life. Our families are very close. In fact, it is expected that Francesca, and I get married one day. If she and I were to break up . . . well, let's just say that our families would be very upset. It would not be something they would find acceptable."

"Are you and Francesca engaged?"

"No. I have not proposed because I do not believe I am in love with Francesca. I love her. I mean, we have been friends since birth. But there is no real connection between us. No real passion. Do you know she is attending a fashion show rather than being here with me?"

"I'm sorry," I said. "I know that you said your families would be upset, but if you are not in love with Francesca, if there is no true relationship there . . ."

"Amanda, my family would likely disown me if I left Francesca. And her family would be embarrassed greatly."

"Your family would rather you marry Francesca even though you are not in love with her? I'm sorry, but I don't understand. I know we just met, and that it is not any of my business, but I don't get it. I can understand them being disappointed, maybe even upset. But what about your happiness? What about marrying for love? Not some sense of obligation?"

"I wish it were different. I wish that it were not so complicated. Believe me, I would have broken up with Francesca a long time ago. Perhaps I would have never dated her in the first place. But . . . it is the way it is. I don't know how to explain it any more than that."

"You don't owe me an explanation. I may not understand it, but I do see this is a complicated mess for you. I just don't know what to do about the feelings I am developing for you. Especially knowing that you are developing the same feelings for me."

"I'll understand if you want to leave."

"Is that what you want?" I asked.

"No. I very much want you to stay. I just don't know if I can offer you anything more than my friendship. No matter how much I may desire more."

I wiped a tear from the corner of my eye. I couldn't believe this. I had only met Matteo two days ago. We had spent one afternoon together. We were less than an hour into our afternoon together now, and I felt crushed by what I was hearing. Is there such a thing as love at first sight? I don't know.

I do know that there is a connection between us. A connection that looks like it is stopping at "just friends."

Maybe it is for the best. My vacation ends in another week. I will be going back to California. I have a job to begin at UCLA. Matteo lives in Italy. Long-distance relationships never work.

I have no doubt that he is good filmmaker, but what are the odds he will win the contest and go to Hollywood? Probably not great, statistically speaking.

Matteo wasn't in love with Francesca, but it was a complicated mess. Too complicated and crowded for there to be room for me in all of it. Other than as a friend.

"I'm sorry. Forgive me," Matteo said after a few moments of our silence.

"No. I'm sorry that you feel so trapped. I can't imagine your situation. Matteo, I enjoy being with you. I would rather be your friend then not have you in my life at all."

Matteo tried to smile. It was a half smile. Our conversation had certainly put a bit of a cloud over the evening, but he was being honest about what he was dealing with. Personally, I didn't feel great. But I knew that Matteo was feeling worse. Maybe right now he just needed a friend.

"Come on," I said, "let's go sit down for lunch."

I held out my arm. Matteo looped his arm through mine and we went to our table. Lunch was delicious. As soon as dessert was served, the awards presentations began. Best Student Film was the final award of the evening. It was the one that everyone was waiting for.

I could see the excitement and anticipation in the room. I could see it in Matteo's eyes. How could Francesca not be here for this?

The presenter stepped to the podium.

"E ora, per la presentazione del Miglior Student Film Award. I candidati sono (And now, for the presentation of the Best Student Film Award. The nominees are...)." The presenter read the list of nominees, in alphabetical order by film name.

"E il vincitore è, (And, the winner is)," the presenter said as he opened the sealed envelope. "Roma al tramonto da Matteo Rosetti (Rome at Sunset by Matteo Rosetti)."

The room broke into a standing ovation. I was applauding loudly. Matteo turned to me and gave me a huge hug with a broad smile on his face and a tear running down his cheek. I hugged him back. It was completely natural. It was instinct. Both his hug and mine.

We embraced for a moment as the applause continued around us. But everything seemed to stop. It was just like when we first met at The Villa Aurelia. We were in our own world where it was just the two of us. It was magical.

Matteo moved to the stage and accepted the movie camera shaped statue. He gave a very humble and appreciative acceptance speech. He thanked his professors, classmates, and friends who had taught him, inspired him, and helped the film become a reality. It was in that moment that it dawned on me. None of his family were present. I don't know why I hadn't realized it before.

Matteo finished his speech and returned to our table with his award in hand.

"Congratulations. That was a wonderful acceptance speech. I am so happy for you."

"Grazie, Amanda. I am glad that you are here with me."

"Me too. There is nowhere else I would rather be."

CHAPTER 12

There was reception following the awards luncheon. Afterward, Matteo asked if I would join him for drinks and dessert at the Minerva Roof Garden for sunset.

"That sounds very nice. I'd love to," I replied.

The Minerva Roof Garden sits atop the Grand Hotel de la Minerve. We ordered drinks and dessert and took in the expansive and fascinating view of Rome.

"This is one of the best places in Roma to see the sunset," declared Matteo.

"I can't wait. The view of the city is amazing."

I took a sip of my drink.

"Matteo, can I ask you something?"

"Yes. Anything."

"If you don't want to tell me, it is okay. It really isn't any of my business . . ."

"Amanda, whatever it is, it is okay."

"I couldn't help but notice that your family did not attend the Student Film Awards."

Matteo gave a gentle nod of his head.

"My family thinks that I am wasting my time making movies. They tell me that I should get a proper job. Then get married and have a family. Do what they did."

"I'm sorry."

"You have nothing to apologize for," said Matteo.

"But I feel bad. My family has always been so supportive of me following my passion," I said.

"To study the Classics?"

"Yes. I wish that everyone had that type of support. Everyone should have that support from their family."

"I agree. But that is not the case with my family."

"And you still follow your dreams. You live your passion. I admire that," I said.

"To me, making films is like breathing air. I couldn't live without it."

"And you are, obviously, very good at making films," I said.

"Grazie. I am fortunate to have attended my film school. I had great support from teachers and friends there. I owe so much to them."

"That came through in your acceptance speech. I think you made your professors and friends proud."

"Ah, look," said Matteo as he pointed toward the setting sun.

We watched as the Sun settled below the horizon and cast its final glow of the day over Rome. The hues of yellow turned to orange, and the sky went from blue to black.

"Absolutely beautiful," I commented.

"Sì," said Matteo.

An evening breeze blew across the rooftop garden. There was a slight chill in the air. Matteo removed his suit coat and draped it over my shoulders. We gazed into each other's eyes. Then we kissed. It was soft and sensual, yet full of passion.

"Mi dispiace; I'm sorry," said Matteo.

"Don't be. Matteo, I know what you said earlier. I know that the relationships with Francesca and your family are complex. I know there is probably no realistic future for us, but don't apologize for kissing me."

"Amanda, I can't offer any more than this."

"Matteo, I will take whatever you can offer me. Even if it is just a kiss. Even if it is just this moment."

"Are you sure? I have never done anything like this before. I have never . . . I have never kissed anyone other than Francesca until now."

"I understand. Matteo, feel my heart." I placed Matteo's hand over my heart. "Do you feel that?"

"Sì."

"That is my heart racing because of you. Whatever this is or whatever this can never be, my heart only knows how being with you makes it feel."

Matteo took my other hand and held it to his heart. We stood as we held our hands over each other's beating hearts.

"And do you feel how mine races for you?" Matteo asked.

"Yes," I replied.

We sat and watched the sun slip below the horizon, the sky turn dark, and gazed at the stars. We held hands and talked for hours. After, Matteo drove me to my hotel and gave me a sweet kiss goodnight in the lobby. We didn't speak another word, but out smiles told each other there was much we would need to discuss.

CHAPTER 13

I had fallen asleep not sure what the day would bring. Would Matteo and I only have the two kisses from the night before? Or would our feelings for each other prove so strong that we would find a way to be together? There were so many variables to consider. Chief among them was the fact that Francesca Parisi was, technically, Matteo's girlfriend.

I normally would not have knowingly kissed a man in a relationship. I'm not a cheater and I would not be the woman a man cheated with. But I saw our situation as different. Yes, Matteo has not broken up with Francesca. It is also true it may never happen.

But Matteo is trapped in a relationship not of his choosing. He is not in love with Francesca. He does not want to marry her. He would break up with her if it were not so complicated and bound to ignite family strife.

I'm still hoping he will end it with her. I know there will be consequences for him if he does, but it is the only way that I can see him beyond last night. Maybe it is selfish of me. And maybe kissing Matteo was wrong.

I suppose they are on a break of sorts. But Matteo did not actually break up with Francesca. At best it is a gray area. My head was hurting trying to figure out exactly what to label what we had done. Just like Matteo's relationship with Francesca, it is complicated.

As I sat and had my first cup of coffee, my phone rang. It was Matteo.

"Hello, Matteo," I answered.

"Good morning, Amanda. I wasn't sure if I should call."

"I understand."

"Amanda, I . . ." Matteo began and then paused a few beats. I allowed for the silence as he collected his thoughts. "I have never felt about Francesca the way I feel about you. I know it sounds, what is the word, impulsive. Perhaps even crazy. But it is the truth. At the same time, I feel I am being unfair to you. I don't know what to do."

"This has been amazing," I said. "You are amazing. I have never felt so connected to anyone in all my life. That is the truth. But, Matteo, I . . . I can't do this again with the way things are. I don't want to say this is a mistake. I don't want to say it was wrong. What is wrong is you being in a relationship with Francesca. At the same time . . ."

"Amanda, I know. I am not a perfect man. But I am not a man who cheats. I refuse to feel bad about what we have shared. I've never felt about Francesca as I do you. Never. But I know that I need to make a decision."

"But you are not prepared to make it now? Are you?"

"I know what I want to do. I just need to be prepared to live with the consequences."

"And you're not sure that you can? Live with the consequences?"

"My family does not support my dreams. They do not understand I am an artist and the art which I make is on film. They want me to be part of the family wine business. To marry Francesca and give them grandchildren."

Matteo paused a few beats. "They are my family. I likely would never see them again. Not even my brothers," he said.

"Are you certain that is what would happen?" I asked. "Would it really be that dramatic? I mean, Matteo, this is the twenty-first century."

"They do not care what century it is. Amanda, there is more I need to tell you."

CHAPTER 14

Matteo told me he wanted to explain. He wanted to tell me everything in detail. We agreed it would be best to talk over a lengthy breakfast. I met Matteo in the lobby of my hotel a half hour later.

"Okay, I'm all set," I said. "Where should we eat?"

"The restaurant across the street is nice. They serve a very good breakfast and we can get a quite table," said Matteo.

"Sounds good."

We made our way down to the lobby and out onto the street. We walked to the corner and waited for the light to change. We crossed the street and walked to the restaurant that was located in the middle of the block. It was fairly busy with the breakfast crowd, but we found a table near the back.

We looked over the menus and ordered. Beyond eating breakfast, I had no idea what was going to happen. I really liked Matteo, and I wanted to find a way to make it work. There was no denying the connection between us. It was electric.

However, when you don't know what you are doing, electricity can give you a wicked shock. Then again, handled properly, electricity lights your world. I didn't know whether I was a clueless Do-It-Yourselfer who was in over her head, or a master electrician.

"You need to forgive me," Matteo began, "for how complicated this all is. It should be much simpler. Two people meet and are attracted to each other. They know that they share a passion. When I first gazed upon you, Amanda, I was instantly drawn to you. Then you spoke, and all I knew is that

I wanted to know more about you. Then we touched, and I could not forget that feeling. Such excitement."

"Matteo, I felt all of that too. But what are we going to do? You said you had more to tell me. I think we need to start there."

"Si. Yes. You need to know everything. At least, maybe, it will help you understand the situation better."

"Let's just start with whatever it is I need to know," I said.

Matteo nodded his head in agreement. He took a sip of coffee. Then he began to explain.

"Amanda, my family history is a bit complex. But that history is extremely important in my family. Not so much to me, but definitely to my parents. And it impacts all of their decisions about family relationships."

Our breakfast came. We began to eat as Matteo continued to explain.

"I know you are an expert in ancient Roman civilization," he said to me, "but the root of my situation only goes back as far as the nineteenth century and the granting of titles of nobility by the King of Italy."

"So your family has some claim to Italian nobility?"

"Yes. Well, we did."

"I'm sure that it must have been mentioned in one of my history classes along the way, but I can't say that I am very familiar with the history of Italian nobility. Not like in England or other European countries."

"It is understandable. Royalty and nobility in Italy has quite a different history from most other European countries. Prior to Italian unification in 1861 there was a relatively large nobility across the various regions of Italy. After the unification, the kings of Italy continued to create titles of nobility to eminent Italians, but for all of Italy. The practice continued until the twentieth century when nominations would be made by the Prime Minister of Italy and approved by the Crown."

"So your family was one of those granted titles of nobility?"

"Yes. In the late nineteenth century. My family had become very successful winemakers. With the wealth they became patrons of the arts and gave generously to other charitable causes. We were an influential and prominent family. From that, we were granted noble titles."

"So you are a wealthy nobleman?"

"Not exactly. Yes, my family is still wealthy. But the money does not matter so much to me. It never has. It is why I didn't mention it earlier. And while there is a beautiful art to making wine, it is not my passion as it is for my parents and my brothers. As for being nobility, no. That is no longer the case," said Matteo.

"How did you lose your titles?" I asked.

"It was not just us. It was nobility itself throughout Italy. In 1946 the Kingdom of Italy was replaced by a republic. Under the Italian Constitution adopted in 1948, titles of nobility were no longer legally recognized. This was definitively affirmed by a high court in 1967. It stated that noble titles granted during the Kingdom of Italy between 1861 and 1946 were no longer law in Italy."

"So your family lost titles of nobility and some sense of family identity and legacy?"

"In a manner of speaking, yes. My parents were born after all of this, but my grandparents remember. They felt a sense of loss for the family. We still had our wealth and prominence, but it still felt like a loss for them. My grandparents feel that even though they cannot lay any legal claim to their titles of nobility that it is part of who they are. They have instilled that in my parents. My parents have tried to instill that in their children."

Matteo stopped to take a bite of his food. I knew there was more he wanted to tell me. I assumed that all of this somehow connected to Francesca. I waited for him to be ready to continue. So I ate and tried to make sense of it all.

"Francesca's family was in the same situation. For our families, marriage between Francesca and I seem to represent an acknowledgment of our histories and a way to keep it alive for the next generation. It means nothing legally, but as long as it means something to our families . . ."

"It is something that cannot be ignored," I said.

"That is correct. If I do not marry Francesca, I will lose everything. My family will no longer talk to me and I will lose my family money. I don't care so much about the money. I live simply. I plan to make my living as a filmmaker. But to lose my family . . . I don't know if I can do that."

I had tears in my eyes. The loss of a noble title due to a change in governance and law may not seem like much to me, or Matteo, but it did to his family. It did to Francesca's family. I now better understood why this was so complicated for Matteo.

"Amanda, my heart longs to be with you. My heart also longs for my family. How can I possibly choose?"

"You don't," I replied.

"I don't understand," said Matteo.

"Matteo, I can't ask you to choose." I had tears streaming down my face. "Before it was just leaving a loveless relationship and upset feelings in your family. With time, we could have worked through those issues. But this? . . . I can't be the one to ask you to give up family. This is all too much and too fast."

"Amanda, what are you saying?"

"I don't know. I just don't know about any of this. I don't see how any of this can work for us. We only just met and we already have these huge obstacles to our starting a relationship. Besides, I live in California and you live here." I wiped the tears on my cheek with the back of my hand. It was futile. The tears were coming faster. My eyes were turning red and puffy.

"Amanda, please don't cry." Matteo reached out his hand and placed it on top of mine.

"Matteo, why can't this all be different?"

"I may win the film internship contest. Then I can come to California."

"But what about Francesca and your family?"

"I don't know. I still need to figure that out," he replied.

"Maybe we just aren't meant to be together," I said.

"Amanda, please, don't say that."

"What else can I say?"

"Not that. I can't ignore what I feel for you," Matteo said.

"I can't ignore my feelings either. They are there. They are real. But that doesn't mean it is going to work for us."

"Let's not make any decisions right now."

"I want this to be different. Believe me, I do. But the longer I stay in hopes that this will work out for us, the harder it will be when it doesn't."

I slid out of the booth and stood. A tear hit the top of the table.

"Amanda, wait."

"Matteo, please. Don't. It will only make it harder."

I leaned over and kissed him on the cheek. I stood straight and turned toward the door. I moved quickly across the restaurant. I pushed open the front door and exited onto the busy Rome sidewalk. I turned and headed back to my hotel – alone.

CHAPTER 15

I had gained some control over my tears by the time I reached the lobby of my hotel. I was a mess, but I was more of a controlled mess. I caught the elevator and punched the button for my floor. Thankfully, I was the only one in the elevator. Most guests were taking in the sites.

The elevator stopped, the doors opened, and I stepped into the hallway on my floor. I turned left and headed down the hall. I found my room key in my bag. As I stepped into my room I was taken by the silence. There was the low hum of the central air cooling the room. Barely even white noise. Other than that, nothing.

I turned on the television. There was a morning talk show. I left it on just to have something in the background. I didn't want to be left alone with just my thoughts. Those were no good to me at the moment. I had made the mistake of falling for a guy while on vacation in Italy.

How stupid could I be? Under normal circumstances it was unlikely to have worked out. I let passion get the better of me. I both refused to regret my time with Matteo and there was a part of me that wished we had never met. Ignorance would have been bliss.

I could have had a spectacular two week vacation in Italy without any drama. I wouldn't have known what I was missing out on. The only problem . . . I did know. Matteo was amazing. We had such a brief time together, but it was going to be hard to get over him. I suppose that one day I would. Today was not that day.

I glanced over at the clock. Eleven o'clock. To early for a drink. I pulled out my cell phone and called Jenny. I couldn't sit in silence, I had no interest in anything on television, and I wasn't sure that I could be a tourist in that moment.

Jenny answered on the third ring.

"Hello," I heard her sleepily say. I just realized that it was only two in the morning in Los Angeles.

"I'm sorry, Jenny. I forgot about the time difference."

"Amanda, what's wrong?"

"Call me later. After you have had a full night of sleep," I said.

"No. It's okay. I'm up now."

"Really sorry," I said.

"Amanda, it's okay. Tell me what is going on."

"I slept with Matteo last night. It was amazing. The passion, Jenny . . . the passion between us was incredible. Beyond incredible."

"I can tell by your voice that isn't the end of the story."

"No. It turns out that he is in a very complicated situation."

"Let me guess, he has a girlfriend? Or is he married?"

"Girlfriend."

"I knew it was a mistake for you to get all ga ga over some guy you just met while on vacation in another country."

"Jenny, it's not quite like that."

"No? You met him the other day. You slept with him last night. Turns out he has a girlfriend. Does that about sum it up?"

"Yes and no."

"What do you mean yes and no? Seems pretty straight forward to me. Amanda, I told you to be careful."

"Jenny, it's more complicated."

"Great. So it's not enough that he has a girlfriend. Wait. He isn't married too, is he?"

"No."

"Not that you know of," said Jenny.

"I'm confident he is not married. He is in a loveless relationship with his girlfriend that, basically, he can't get out of."

"Is that what he told you?"

"Yes. He explained his situation to me," I said.

"And you believed him?"

"Yes. His situation is a difficult one."

"Amanda, are you really that naïve?"

"Who says that I am naïve?"

"Well, let's just look at the facts."

"Jenny, you're not being very sympathetic toward how I'm feeling right now."

"I'm sorry, sweetie. You know that I love you like a sister. Heck, I'm closer to you than I am to my own sister. But you have to admit that this all sounds kinda fishy. If the shoe were on the other foot ..."

"If the shoe were on the other foot, I would listen to everything you have to say and reserve any sort of judgment until I had all the facts," I said.

Jenny was silent for a moment.

"I'm sorry," she said. "You're right. I should hear you out."

"Thank you."

I told her everything that Matteo had told me. She was still a little skeptical, but I insisted that I was convinced that Matteo was sincere. I couldn't fully explain to her the connection that I felt with Matteo. I could only tell her that it was real. And that I was hurting. No matter what she thought about the rest, she fully understood my pain.

"I'm sorry, Amanda. I wish I could just take it all away from you."

"I know you do," I said.

"It may be hard now, but you will get over this," she said. "We've both been through this before and we have both survived. Thrived, even."

"I know that too. This just feels different. I know it sounds crazy to you. In a way, it is crazy to me as well. I just know how I feel."

"You know that I am here for you. Day or night," said Jenny.

"I do. Although, I will try not to call you at two in the morning next time."

"It doesn't matter. I'm always available for you. Listen, I'm going to call you later to check in. Okay?" said Jenny.

"That would be great. Thanks."

"No need to thank me. I'll call you later. Just promise me that you will get out of your hotel room and do something fun today. Be all nerdy classics person and see some ancient ruins or something."

"I'll think about doing that. I hope you can get back to sleep."

"You know me. My head hits the pillow and I'm out. I'll power sleep for the next five hours."

"Talk to you later. Good night."

"Get out and see Rome," Jenny said before she hung up.

I walked over to the window and looked out. Residents and tourists of Rome were going about their day. I considered what Jenny said. She was right. Sitting in my hotel room wasn't going to make me feel any better. I tossed my phone, wallet, and travel guide into my small backpack and headed out the door.

CHAPTER 16

Matteo

Matteo watched Amanda walk out of the restaurant and out of his life. He didn't know what else to do. Amanda wasn't going to make him choose. She had made the decision for them. He sat and thought about what had just transpired. Could he have risked never seeing his family again to be with her?

Matteo's phone vibrated in his back pocket. He leaned forward and pulled his phone out. He glanced at the screen. His brother Lorenzo had texted him.

Lorenzo: Getting together with Marco, Davide, &
Giovanni at Martinelli's tonight. You coming?

Lorenzo was Matteo's older brother by two years. Marco was his younger brother by a year. Davide and Giovanni Martinelli were friends of the Rosetti brothers. Davide was Lorenzo's age and Giovanni was an even six months between Matteo and Marco. Davide and Giovanni's parents owned a restaurant that had been a hang out of the five since childhood.

Matteo thought about whether he just wanted to be alone. He decided that it would be good to see his brothers and friends. Maybe they would have some wisdom to impart on him. Probably not, he thought to himself. But it was better than being alone.

Matteo: I'll be there.
Lorenzo: 7:00
Matteo: OK

Matteo paid the check from breakfast. He stood up and traced Amanda's steps out of the restaurant. When he was outside he paused and looked over at her hotel. He tried to count the floors and figure out which window belonged to her room. He narrowed it down to three. Beyond that, he wasn't sure. Besides, the room was too far up to be able to see anything.

He turned and walked to the corner and crossed with the light. He continued straight past the hotel to the parking garage. He climbed to the second level and located his car. He put the top down on the Fiat Spider and then got in. He noticed Amanda's sunglasses sitting on the passenger seat.

He picked the sunglasses up off the seat. He got out of the car and went to the lobby. He handed them to the front desk clerk and asked that they be returned to Amanda's room. As he crossed the lobby back toward the parking garage, he thought that he saw Amanda exiting the hotel.

Matteo continued back to his car. He got in and started the engine. He pulled out of the parking space and drove down to the first level. He stopped and paid the attendant. Then he exited the hotel parking garage. He turned left and raced off down the street. He had no destination in mind. He just needed to drive and clear his head.

Matteo headed out of Rome. He got on route A24 and just drove. He left the city behind. He passed through the suburbs and into the hilly countryside. The hot July sun beat down, and the breeze whipped through his wavy black hair. After an hour, Matteo reached a small town. He found a store and purchased a Coke.

He sat on the hood of his car and drank the soda. Why couldn't he and Amanda just run off somewhere together? Anywhere? Then he thought about his parents, and Lorenzo, and Marco. Family.

He figured that winning the Pacific Coast Pictures contest was a long shot. Others had told him that he was a leading contender. He didn't think so. If he did win, however, he and Amanda could be together in California. He could put off marrying Francesca.

Why didn't you say that to Amanda?, he asked himself. No good reason. He hadn't been able to think straight since meeting her. *Why is your family life so damn complicated?*, he thought.

If he could win the contest, or find another way to get to California, maybe over time he could convince his parents that he was in love with Amanda. *Are you in love with her?*, he thought to himself. Matteo wasn't sure.

We only just met, he thought. Maybe it was too soon to call it love. Perhaps. But there was more passion than anything he had ever felt toward Francesca.

"How could you just let her walk out of the restaurant?" he said to himself out loud. Matteo didn't have a good answer for that either. Lots of questions. No good answers.

Matteo finished his coke and dropped the empty bottle into a recycling bin. He checked his watch. It was a little after Noon. He had figured as much. The sun was directly above in the sky. He got in his car and headed back to Rome.

CHAPTER 17

After Matteo had returned to Rome, he stopped by Pietro's and they went over the filming schedule for the following week. Pietro asked Matteo about Amanda and what had happened with Francesca. Matteo gave him a Cliff Notes version and told Pietro that he really didn't want to talk about it. Matteo and Pietro were friends from film school, but not close friends. The Cliff Notes version was enough to satisfy them both on the topic of Amanda and Francesca.

At 6:45, Matteo headed over to Martinelli's. He arrived just a little past seven. He parked and went in to find Lorenzo, Marco, Davide, and Giovanni at their usual table. Matteo walked over and took the empty chair next to Marco.

"What will you have?" asked Davide.

"Usual," answered Matteo.

Davide waived one of the waiters over and placed Matteo's order. Fettuccine Alfredo. They were all sharing a large appetizer of Bruschetta.

"Where have you been hiding yourself the past few weeks?" asked Giovanni.

"I've been working on and independent film. I also had the Student Film Awards last night."

"How did that go?" asked Davide.

"I won for best film," replied Matteo.

"Congratulazioni (congratulations)!" said Davide. Giovanni followed suit.

"Yeah, congrats," said Marco.

"We're proud of you, Matteo. I'm sorry that we couldn't attend. You know . . ."

"I know. Momma (*Mom*) and Papa (*Dad*) wouldn't let you. It's why I didn't even say anything about it."

"Did you tell them that you won?"

"No. What's the point? They would make some comment about how a student film award does nothing in helping to produce and sell wine."

"Hey, how's Francesca?" asked Giovanni, trying to change the subject.

"Fine. I guess. We're sorta on a break right now."

"A break? What is that supposed to mean?" asked Lorenzo.

"Just what I said. A break. We're still together, but taking a few days apart from each other. To think things over."

"You're not actually thinking of breaking up with her, are you?" asked Marco.

Matteo simply shrugged his shoulders.

"You can't be even remotely serious about that," said Lorenzo.

"If I'm honest with you guys, can you promise not to say anything to anyone about what I am about to tell you?" asked Matteo.

Lorenzo, Marco, Davide, and Giovanni all looked at each other.

"You have to promise," said Matteo.

"We promise," answered Lorenzo.

Matteo looked at Marco, Davide, and Giovanni. They all nodded their heads in agreement.

"Okay. I don't love her. Not in the way you should love someone that you have dated practically your entire life.

Certainly not the way you love someone that everyone expects you to marry."

"That would explain why you haven't proposed to her," said Lorenzo. "I always figured you were just waiting to finish film school."

"She is self-absorbed and has no real interests. We have nothing in common."

"Matteo, you know how Momma and Papa feel about you marrying Francesca," said Lorenzo. "First, they wouldn't understand how you could not love her. It's just assumed that you two were meant to be in love with each other. Second, I'm not sure that they would care. They would simply say that you will grow to love her. Especially once you have children together. End of discussion."

"Don't you think I know that?" said Matteo. "It's all I have heard my whole life. How Francesca and I being born two days apart was some sort of sign. How we could pass the noble blood lines of the Rosetti's and Parisi's to another generation. Even though noble titles haven't been recognized in over six decades."

"I get it, Matteo. Marco and I both get it, but Momma and Papa made a promise to Nonna and Nonno (*Grandma* and *Grandpa*) that at least one of us would marry a Parisi. Francesca is the only Parisi girl. You two are the same age. You won by default."

"Lost, you mean," said Matteo.

"If you break up with her," said Marco, "you know what they will do."

"What will they do?" asked Davide.

The Rosetti boys had grown up with the Martinelli boys, but they had never discussed the Rosetti family feelings around Matteo and Francesca marrying. Everyone always just assumed they were so close growing up and fell in love. Matteo had questioned it once as a boy. His parents made it very clear what their position on the matter was. Matteo never asked again.

"They'll cut me off," replied Matteo.

"Your money?" asked Davide.

"Everything. Everybody."

"What do you mean?" asked Giovanni.

"They wouldn't let me see any family. They would take my trust fund away."

"Seriously?" asked Davide.

Matteo, Lorenzo, and Marco all nodded their heads.

"Wow," replied Davide.

"Yeah," added Giovanni.

"But you guys would still find a way? Right?" asked Davide.

"To see each other?" asked Lorenzo.

"Yeah. I mean, come on, you're brothers. You're grown men," said David.

"We've never talked about it," answered Lorenzo. "I guess we never considered Matteo may not want to marry Francesca."

"Well, now it looks like that is something you need to consider," said Giovanni.

"There's more," said Matteo. "I've met someone."

Lorenzo, Marco, Davide, and Giovanni all looked at Matteo. Four pairs of eyes staring at him. Waiting for him to elaborate.

"She's an American. We just met, but I have never felt this way before. Not about anyone. Certainly not Francesca."

"Is she living in Rome?" asked Lorenzo.

"No. She's a professor at the University of California in Los Angeles. Or, she will be. She just got her PhD. She was here teaching a course at the American Academy."

"Matteo, how can you even think about dating someone else? Let alone someone that doesn't even live in Italy?" asked Lorenzo. Ever the older brother.

"I didn't think about it," answered Matteo. "I felt it. We had an instant connection. There is a passion there that is stronger than anything any of us have ever felt for a woman. And it's real."

"This isn't some romance book or movie, Matteo," said Marco. "There is no way you can make this work."

"She didn't even give me that option. She told me that she couldn't make me choose between family and her."

"I don't want to sound crass, little brother, but problem solved," said Lorenzo.

"It's for the best," added Marco.

"No. It isn't problem solved. It isn't for the best. Not even remotely close," said Matteo.

"Are you saying that you would actually consider leaving Francesca for this woman? That you would toss your family aside for this? Matteo, you need to get your head on straight," said Lorenzo.

"I don't want to be with Francesca. That would be the case even if I had not met Amanda."

"Okay," said Lorenzo. "But the result is the same either way. You leave Francesca and it is game over. No matter whether you leave her to be alone or to be with this, Amanda, or for someone else. It doesn't matter. You leave Francesca and

Momma and Papa will force you leave us as well. You give everything up."

"What if I were in love with Amanda? Don't you think that would count for something?" asked Matteo. He already knew the answer, but he had to ask just the same.

"It should. But it won't," answered Lorenzo.

"I agree," said Marco. "You know what Momma and Papa are like. Especially Papa. No way this has an outcome that you might want."

"So I am just supposed to marry Francesca and live in a loveless marriage and procreate just to satisfy their sense of our family nobility? A nobility that no one, except them, even recognizes anymore? Is that what you want for me?!"

The table grew silent. Davide and Giovanni had become spectators of the Rosetti brother discussion. Lorenzo and Marco had already said what they knew they were supposed to say. Was there anything else left to say?

Dinner arrived. After the waiter left, everyone just stared at the dishes in front of them. After a few beats more of silence, Lorenzo spoke.

"Talk to Momma and Papa. It's all you can do," he said. "Unless you just stay with Francesca."

"I don't think that I can stay with Francesca," said Matteo.

"Then talk to Momma and Papa. But try to speak with Momma first. Marco and I will speak to them as well," said Lorenzo.

"We will?" Marco asked.

"Yes. Giovanni is right. We are brothers. We are grown men now. We need to at least help Matteo make the case to Momma and Papa," replied Lorenzo.

"Okay," said Marco. He was less sure about confronting his parents, but he would follow Lorenzo's lead.

"We good, Matteo?" asked Lorenzo.

Matteo gave a half-hearted nod of the head. There was nothing more to be said by the Rosetti brothers. Lorenzo was right. Matteo could either accept his fate as it had been delivered to him or talk to his parents. The third option, which Lorenzo didn't even offer, was a nuclear option. Matteo could leave Francesca no matter what.

CHAPTER 18

Matteo wasn't very hungry. He had Martinelli's box up his Fettuccine Alfredo. He'd heat it up and eat later. Assuming he had an appetite later. He walked to his car in the cooler evening air. When he reached his Fiat he got in. Even after starting the car, he wasn't sure where he was going. After a minute, he pulled away from the curb and headed toward his parents house.

He arrived fifteen minutes later. He sat outside for a few minutes trying to get up the nerve to go in.

"Matteo, is that you?" called his mother from the front of the house.

"Sì, Momma."

"Why are you sitting in your car? Come in."

Matteo got out and crossed the driveway. He kissed his mother on the cheek. She gave him a hug and a kiss.

"What brings you over this time of night?" she asked.

"Momma, I need to speak with you about something."

"Alright. Let me get your father."

"No. I want to speak with you first. Alone."

"Sounds serious."

"It is."

"Okay. Come, sit here with me."

Mrs. Rosetti sat on the front stoop. Matteo sat next to her. Matteo was silent was for a few moments.

"Matteo, what is it?" asked his mother.

"It's about Francesca," he said.

"Is she alright?"

"Yes. She is fine."

"Then what is it?"

"Momma I don't want you to be upset . . ."

"I don't like where this is going," she said. "Perhaps I should get Papa."

"No. Please," pleaded Matteo. "I need to speak with you first."

"Your father and I don't make decisions without each other. You know that. I'm not sure that I am comfortable with this."

"Momma, please. Just give me a moment to hear me out."

Mrs. Rosetti sat in silence looking at her second son. Matteo knew he could continue.

"Momma, I know how hard this will be for you to hear. It is hard for me to say."

Mrs. Rosetti focused intently on Matteo. It was if she wanted to be absolutely certain that she could see the words come out of his mouth as he said them.

"Things are not going well between us. I . . . I . . . I don't know if we can stay together."

There. He said it. At least part of it. But it was a start.

Mrs. Rosetti patted Matteo's hand.

"Matteo, dear, every couple goes through a rough patch. It is normal. The two of you will figure it out. Young love conquers all."

"That's just it. I'm not in love with Francesca."

"What?! No. That is not possible. You and Francesca have been inseparable since birth. You two are destined to marry. She is your soul mate."

"No. Momma, she is not. I don't love her. I have never loved her. As a friend, yes. But never romantically. I don't think that she truly loves me either."

"Did she tell you that?"

"Not in so many words."

"Then how do you know that she doesn't love you?"

"I just know."

"Matteo, this is nonsense. This even surpasses your silly notion of being a filmmaker. Now, you have had your film experience. You are done with school now. It is time for you to come work with your brothers at the winery. Ask Francesca to marry you. We can plan a big, wonderful, wedding. Then . . . then you can get to work on making us some grandchildren."

"Momma, you aren't listening to a thing that I am saying. You never have."

"Matteo, how dare you say that?!"

"Because it is true. I mean no disrespect, but you and Papa never listen to me."

"You speak and words come out? Did I not just hear them?"

"You hear what you want to hear. Not the truth."

Matteo's father came to the front door.

"What's going on? Oh, is that Matteo?"

"Hello, Papa."

"What brings you here?"

"He says he doesn't love Francesca. That they are not in love."

"What?!"

Matteo's father stepped outside with his wife and son.

"Did you have a fight?" Mr. Rosetti asked Matteo.

"Yes. But not today. The fact of the matter is we don't get along most of the time. Papa, I don't love her. She doesn't love me. It is a relationship of . . . I don't know what it is. But it's not real. It never has been."

"This is utter nonsense," said Mr. Rosetti.

"See," Matteo said to his mother. "This is what I am talking about. You two made up your minds twenty-five years ago about who I could love. Who I could marry. You haven't deviated from that once my whole life."

"Have you been drinking? Are you on drugs?" Mr. Rosetti asked.

"Papa, no."

"At least that would explain your behavior. What's your excuse, then?"

"My excuse? My excuse is that I am not in love with Francesca."

"She's a beautiful girl," Mr. Rosetti said.

"The two of you will make beautiful babies together," added Mrs. Rosetti.

"Yes, Francesca is beautiful. There is no denying that. And I am sure that any children she may have will be equally attractive. But I don't want her to have those children with me. I'm not in love with her. I won't be happy if I marry her. What kind of husband could I possibly make if I don't love my wife?"

"You will be a husband of noble blood who is married to a woman of noble blood. Your children will have that noble blood flowing in their veins." Mr. Rosetti replied.

"People stopped recognizing the nobility before you were even born. My generation is so far removed from that . . ."

Matteo's father slapped him across the face.

"How dare you disrespect us like this?!"

"Momma, Papa. I mean no disrespect. It is just fact. I get that the Rosettis and the Parisis have a heritage from nobility. From when the King of Italy granted such a thing to prominent families in Italy. I know how great our two families were in the eyes of the king. But, Papa, we were great because of who are families were as people and what our families did to help make Italy great. We received noble titles because of that. We weren't great because of the titles."

Mr. Rosetti sat on the stoop next to his wife. He rubbed his hand through his thick, wavy hair. Thick and wavy, like Matteo's. Except Mr. Rosetti's was now more white than black.

"I have known Mr. Parisi since I was a boy. Our parents talked about how wonderful it would be to join our two noble families through marriage. You and Francesca represented that opportunity. They would be disgraced if you were to reject Francesca Parisi."

"I respectfully disagree," said Matteo. "They would be disgraced if I married Francesca without loving her. How would that honor the great names of our families?"

"Momma, Papa. I love you. And I love Lorenzo and Marco. And you know how much I loved Nanna and Nanno. I don't know how I could live without my family. But I don't know how I can live with Francesca."

"You have made your case," said Mr. Rosetti.

"You know how much family means to me," said Matteo. "Please don't make me choose between marrying a woman I don't love or . . ."

"We've said enough for one night," said Mr. Rosetti.

Mr. and Mrs. Rosetti stood. They stepped through the front door of their house.

"Goodnight, Figlio (*Son*)," said Mr. Rosetti.

Matteo's parents closed the door. Matteo turned and walked toward his car. He got in and started the engine. He pulled out of the driveway and turned up the street and away from his parents house. For the third time that day, he wasn't sure exactly where he was headed.

CHAPTER 19

Matteo found himself parked outside Francesca's apartment. There was a hint of light around the edges of the living room curtains. He was surprised that she was not out partying at some local club. Perhaps she and some girlfriends were partying in the apartment. No. It was too quite for a party.

Was it possible Francesca was sitting and contemplating all that was so terribly wrong with their so-called relationship? *Not likely*, Matteo thought. He wasn't superstitious, nor was he all that sure about destiny or fate. But he reasoned that Francesca being home meant, at the very least, that he needed to go through with talking to her. *That is why you drove over here, isn't it?* He asked himself.

Matteo sat in his car a while longer. He realized that he had spent a lot of time in his car that day thinking. Both driving and parked. Matteo was beginning to feel a little creepy after watching the apartment for several minutes.

You either need to go in there or leave, he told himself. He placed his hand on the key. He was about to turn it to start the engine. Then he removed his hand. He placed his hand back on the key. This time he pulled it out of the ignition.

Matteo got out of the car and walked to the front door. He knocked. Francesca opened the door, and he stepped into the small living room.

"Matteo, you have come to your senses," she said.

Matteo didn't say a word. He was still gathering his thoughts in his head. He wanted to be very clear about what he would say.

"How could you not come back?" Francesca continued. "You could never do better than me."

"I'm not in love with you," Matteo said.

"Mi scusi? (*Excuse me*)?"

"Francesca, I love you. As a friend. Maybe even like a sister. But I am not in love with you. There's a difference."

"What are you saying?"

"Francesca, we are not going to start with that again."

Francesca stepped directly in front of Matteo. She wrapped her arms around him. Matteo pulled away. She pressed in more forcefully.

"Don't you want to kiss me?" she asked.

"Didn't you hear what I just said?"

"You are tired and not thinking clearly."

Francesca kissed Matteo. He pulled away from her.

"Stop," he said.

Matteo stepped toward the sofa. He wanted to be out of striking distance. Francesca had a fiery temper. Her blows didn't necessarily hurt, but he preferred not to get hit all the same.

"Francesca, I want to make our break permanent. I'm sorry, but I'm not in love with you. We can't stay together."

Francesca's eyes grew wide and her nostrils flared. She was a beautiful woman, but that was not her most becoming look.

"What did you just say?"

"Look, I don't want this to be bitter or ugly. We aren't right for each other. We both know that."

"So you are leaving me?"

"I'm breaking up with you. Leaving would imply that we were ever really together."

"No!" Francesca shouted.

"I'm sorry, Francesca."

"You are finished, Matteo! Ruined! You will have no family! And when my family learns of this . . . the Parisis will no longer associate with the Rosettis."

"Francesca, I understand that you are upset . . ."

"I have devoted my life to you. For what? I figured you would get over your stupid films and get a real job at your family's winery. You know, be like your brothers. Then we would marry and have children."

"You weren't all that devoted."

"Why are you being so cruel?"

"I am not trying to be cruel. Francesca, for the first time in our lives, I am being honest about us. I don't think you are in love with me any more than I am with you. We had the idea of being in love planted in our heads by our parents. Drummed into us from birth. Maybe for a while we tried to believe that it was true. . . . Maybe you tried to believe it longer than I did."

"My parents told me to act as if I loved you and that one day I would," said Francesca.

"Did you? Actually fall in love?"

"No. But this is who we are supposed to be," she said.

"I would have been surprised if you had said yes," Matteo said. "You never showed any real interest in me or in having a real relationship."

Francesca sat on the sofa. She turned away from Matteo. He couldn't tell if she was starting to cry or preparing to strike like a coiled snake. Maybe both.

"I don't want to hurt you," he said. "I also don't want to continue to live a lie. It's not fair to either one of us."

"What am I supposed to do?" asked Francesca. "My life was to marry you. I don't think I can do anything else."

"So that was the plan? Marry me even though you are not in love with me? Have children with me even though we have no relationship?"

"There are people who live like that," she replied.

"But is that what you want for your life? Is that the type of household you would want to raise children in?"

"Just leave," she said. "Go!"

"Francesca, I want you to be happy too. Truly happy. We may have had some fun, but I don't think either one of us can say that we were ever truly happy together."

Francesca walked past him into the bedroom. She closed the bedroom door.

"Goodbye, Francesca," Matteo said softly. He walked across the living room and exited the apartment.

Matteo walked to his car and got in. He started the engine and pulled away from the curb. This time, he knew exactly where he was going.

CHAPTER 20

Amanda

I had a full day just being a tourist. I visited the Roman Forum and the Pantheon. The Pantheon was remarkably intact considering that it was built in 27 B.C.. After the Pantheon I had stopped at a cafe for a cappuccino. I thought that we had a lot of coffee shops in the United States, but I think that coffee is Rome's most important drink.

After my cappuccino I strolled through some shops. After window shopping, I had dinner at a small restaurant around the corner from my hotel. The morning had emotionally drained me, but I had managed to get through the day. I even enjoyed moments of it.

Back in my hotel room, I took a bubble bath until the water had turned cold. I stepped out of the tub looking as wrinkled as a prune. I toweled off and put on a pair of comfortable pajamas. I padded over to the bed and pulled my kindle out of my suitcase. I climbed under the sheets and settled in for some lite reading.

I was hoping that the book would be enough of a distraction until I was ready to fall asleep. I was almost through one day. Tomorrow I would try to get through one more. Then, I hoped, it would start to get a little easier.

How many days does it take to get over someone you just met? *Did I even want to get over it?* I asked myself. I walked away because . . . *why did I walk away?* I guess because it seemed like the practical thing to do. Matteo stood to lose too much for the chance at a relationship with me. But I made the decision for him. Maybe that was wrong.

Had I been too hasty or rash in my decision? Isn't Matteo capable of making his own decisions? It suddenly dawned on me that I may have made a huge mistake. Yes, it was complicated. Yes, we live over 6,000 miles apart. Yes, we only just met.

I was good at making lists. I could sit all night and come up with any number of reasons why a relationship with Matteo wasn't practical. Why it didn't make a lot of sense. I had compiled and analyzed that list in rapid fashion over breakfast. It led me to the only conclusion that made sense in that moment.

The only problem is that I failed to make another list. The list with only one thing on it: Matteo and I had feelings for each other that were beyond anything either of us had ever felt before. And that singular item should have been the only one that mattered.

Just then there was a knock at my door. It was late. I figured that someone had the wrong room. I padded over to the door and peeked through the security hole. I couldn't believe it. I threw off the security latch and opened the door.

"Matteo," I said.

"I know it is late . . ."

"I'm still up. Come in."

Matteo stepped in and I closed the door behind him.

"I know what you said this morning, but I had to see you."

"I know what I said, too. I may have been a bit hasty. I was, in fact, hasty. I want a do over."

"I like the sounds of a do over," he said.

He appeared tired and emotionally drained, but he also seemed relieved. A day of difficulty that had given him some peace. And even in the shadow of the dimly lit foyer, Matteo was breathtakingly handsome. Just him standing there stirred excitement within me.

"Matteo, I was wrong earlier. I know that this is hard, but most things that truly matter in life don't come easy. At any rate, I shouldn't have just walked away. I only saw how difficult our situation is. I didn't look at what should have mattered most. I don't know if this can work, but walking out of the restaurant this morning didn't even give us a chance to find out."

"I am sorry that we were even in that position," said Matteo.

"You have nothing to apologize for. This must be incredibly hard for you. I guess part of me didn't want to force you into a decision that could have such a dramatic impact on your life."

"I understand. Amanda, I have done a lot of thinking today. I drove out into the country and back. I spoke with my brothers, and my parents, and Francesca. I'm not sure that anything has changed with my parents, but I did break up with Francesca. For good. No matter what happens between us, I can't continue to live that lie. But I do want a chance for us to figure out how this might work between us."

I wrapped my arms around Matteo and hugged him. He pulled me close, and we held on to each other. Then he looked into my eyes. His eyes sparkled. They were vibrant and joyful.

"I still don't know how my parents will react when they learn that I am no longer with Francesca. But I already told them that I am not in love with her and do not want to marry her. They know I have been unhappy. They gave no real indication of what they might do, but that is not an entirely bad thing," he said.

"Because they did not tell you that you must stay with her or else?"

"Yes. Perhaps there is hope. Plus, my brothers understand and they will also speak to my parents on my behalf. But, Amanda, I can't control any of that now. Whatever happens now, happens. But I have made the decision to not stay trapped in a relationship that meant nothing to me."

"Matteo, I am happy that you are free of that. I only hope things will work out with your family. And I know that we still have to figure out what happens between us when my vacation is over next week."

"And we will," said Matteo. "There must be a way. Even if I don't win the contest, I will find a way to get to California. That has always been my dream. And now, my dream includes being there with you."

CHAPTER 21

Matteo

Matteo woke with thoughts of Amanda's warm lips on his own. Visions of her soft skin danced in his mind. Then he frowned. He had been summoned to his parents house for breakfast. He did not know what to expect, but he knew his position and was determined to stand up for himself.

Matteo's mother had prepared a freshly cooked breakfast. Matteo poured himself a cup of steaming espresso. He sat with Lorenzo and Marco at the table on the patio. Their parents sat at either end. Mr. Rosetti showed no emotion. Mrs. Rosetti seemed happy to have all three of her boys sitting at the table with them.

"Matteo, your brothers came and spoke with us last evening. Just after you left," said Mr. Rosetti.

"Papa, may I say something?" asked Matteo.

Mr. Rosetti nodded his head for Matteo to speak.

"I don't know what you are about to say, but I need for you all to know how much I love you. I know that you do not support my being a filmmaker. I know how much you have wanted for me to marry Francesca. And I know that has put something between us. But I love you. I love this family. I don't want to ever not be part of this family. But I could no longer live a lie. I broke up with Francesca last night. I know you will be disappointed, but it was the best thing to do. Francesca isn't in love with me any more than I am with her."

Mr. Rosetti held up his hand. The universal signal for stop. Matteo swallowed hard.

"We know," Mr. Rosetti said. "The Parisi's called last night. Francesca was upset, not because she lost a love, but because she is unsure what to do now. That, Son, is not your fault. We see now that you two were never in love. I love your mother and, on most days, your mother loves me."

Mrs. Rosetti tossed a breakfast roll at her husband.

"Francisco, you stop. I love you every day. I have for over forty years," she said.

"See, even after all these years, still feisty and playful," said Mr. Rosetti. "That was one of the first things that I fell in love with about your Momma."

"What your Papa is trying to say, dear, is that we want all of our boys to marry for love. Yes, we very much tried to will you and Francesca to be together. The tradition of nobility loomed large in that hopeful desire. But, in the end, you are right. If the two of you are not in love, then you shouldn't be together," said Mrs. Rosetti.

"Momma, Papa, I can't believe what I am hearing," exclaimed Matteo with a broad smile on his face.

"Well, I believe that Nonna and Nonno would understand," said Mr. Rosetti. "They loved you. They loved all of you boys very much. Sometimes we want something so much for our children, or grandchildren, that we can become blinded to what is really going on. It seemed perfect when you and Francesca were born. We were trying to create a reality that did not exist. Now, let's eat this wonderful breakfast that your Momma made."

"Francisco," said Mrs. Rosetti, "Isn't there something else to say to Matteo?" It was more of a reminder than a question.

"Oh, right." Mr. Rosetti paused a beat. "Matteo, one of the professors over at the film school sent us a DVD of your final film project, Rome at Sunset . . ."

"It was a beautiful film," interjected Mrs. Rosetti. She was beaming.

Is my mother actually proud of the film that I made?, Matteo asked himself.

"Si. We can see why it won Best Student Film. Why you won," said Mr. Rosetti.

"We are sorry we were not there to see you win that award," added Mrs. Rosetti. "We are sorry that we have not supported your film making."

"You make better films than you do wine," said Mr. Rosetti. They all laughed.

"Si. The wine you made tasted like pee," cackled Marco.

"It wasn't that bad," said Mrs. Rosetti.

"Yes, it was," said Lorenzo.

"I agree," said Matteo. "That is what I have been trying to say all these years. I have no business being in the wine business."

"Well, I still think that you sabotaged your keg on purpose," said Mr. Rosetti.

"Papa, no!" exclaimed Matteo jokingly.

Matteo could not remember the last time his entire family laughed and joked together. He could not remember when they were all truly happy to be together and that he felt the love and support of his parents. But as laughter surrounded the table, he smiled. Matteo was more than free, he was hopeful and confident about his future.

CHAPTER 22

Amanda

Matteo returned to the hotel and told me about breakfast with his family. I couldn't believe the change in his parents' attitude. I was also very relieved. We still needed to figure out how we were going to make our relationship work after I returned to California, but international logistics seemed minor compared to what we had been facing.

We spent the afternoon touring parts of Rome that are not well known to most tourists. It was fabulous. Matteo gave me a glimpse at Roman culture that can only come from someone who knows the city as well as he does. That evening we got dressed up for a romantic dinner.

We dined by candlelight and enjoyed the most amazing meal. We strolled arm-in-arm across the square that separated the restaurant and my hotel. The night air was a perfect temperature for a leisurely stroll by moonlight. As we approached the square's fountain, Matteo stopped. He pulled some change out of his pocket.

"Lore has it that if you throw change into the fountain that you will find love before you leave Rome," he said.

I took the change from his hand and tossed all of it into the fountain. The coins landed with a splash.

"How long do you have to wait?" I asked.

"That depends," he replied.

"On what?" I asked.

"How ready you are to find love."

I leaned in and kissed him. "Ready enough?" I asked.

CHAPTER 23

Two espressos and a full breakfast fueled me for my morning of sight seeing. Matteo had sent me a text that he had an unexpected lunch with his brothers to go over some family business. He had told me that it was no big deal, nothing to worry about. He said that he would meet up with me. His most recent text told me that he had finished lunch and where should he meet me.

I was just finishing a quick lunch at a cafe off of Piazza Campidoglio. I had spent the morning at the Palazzo dei Conservatori Museum. I gave Matteo the cafe's name and address. Fifteen minutes later I saw him cross the square. I was sitting on the outside patio, so I was easy to spot.

"Ciao," he said. He kissed me on the cheek and pulled out the chair opposite me at the table. The waitresses came over and asked if she could get him anything. He asked for a glass of water with lemon. She seemed disappointed at not adding to the bill, but returned a moment later with his glass of water.

Matteo forced a smile. He shifted uncomfortably in his chair. I could hear his feet shuffling under the table. Nervous energy.

"What's wrong? Did something happen at lunch with your brothers?" I asked.

He wasn't even trying to force the smile any longer. It had given way to a rather solemn look. It was a sunny and warm July day in Rome, but I felt as if a dark cloud had just moved in over our table.

"Matteo, what is going on? You can tell me." My tone expressed both concern and a plea. Anyone could see that Matteo was upset. That was enough to worry me. That he seemed reluctant to share was even more troubling.

His eyes shifted toward me. He was attempting to make eye contact, but seemed, I don't know, almost fearful to do so. The news had to be very bad for me. For us. I was beginning to think that it had nothing to do with family business. Matteo pursed his lips. He took a sip of water.

"I received a letter from Pacific Coast Pictures. I did not win the internship and scholarship to USC."

"Matteo, I'm sorry. Wait, Pacific Coast Pictures? That's where my best friend, Jenny, works. Maybe I can –"

"No. Whoever won deserved to win. They made a better film than me."

"Just because they won, doesn't mean the film was better."

Matteo shifted his eyes away and then back. But his head was tilted so that he was not looking at me directly. I reached out my hand and placed it under his chin. I gently turned his face toward me.

"So it means you won't be coming to California? You will need to stay here?" It was more of a statement than a question. It seemed obvious. It seemed like the only thing that Matteo could do in the situation. He simply nodded his head.

"And what about us?" I asked.

"I don't know," Matteo replied. "I want to be with you. I want to discover if we can build something together. I just don't know how we do that if you are in California and I am here in Italy."

"Are you telling me that it is over? Would it be easier for us to say goodbye now? I walked away too easily before. I know that it doesn't make it any easier. Not for me. Not for us. I don't want to do that again," I said.

We were both silent again for a few minutes. The waitress came with the check. Matteo offered to pay. I waived him off and left ten euros. Enough for my meal and a generous tip.

"Matteo, I still have a week left in Italy. Perhaps we should not make any rash decisions. It will give us time to think about what to do next. In the meantime, we have a week together." I would have preferred to have everything wrapped up with a nice bow, but our short history was not like that. Maybe I was deciding to embrace the unknown.

"You know," I said, "we can actually make this fun."

Matteo cocked his head and gave me a look that suggested I was certifiably crazy. Okay, he wasn't sold just yet. So I continued.

"We don't know what is going to happen in the future. It remains to be seen how we will make it all work. But we do know we have a week. What is the most fun we can have together in a week?"

I ran my finger along Matteo's arm. The corners of his mouth started to curl upward. The beginnings of a smile.

"Have you ever been to Venice?" he asked me.

"No. I figured I would get there on my next to trip to Italy," I replied.

"My family has an apartment in Venice. What would you think of visiting now? We can get away. Just the two of us," he said.

"Leave everything behind for a week," I said.

"A week just devoted to us."

"What about your film schedule?" I asked.

"I will let Pietro handle things. He is the Assistant Director. He can take over for a few days."

"Okay," I said. "Let's go to Venice."

CHAPTER 24

We made reservations on the Eurail for the following morning. Matteo suggested that we stop in Verona for a day and then go on to Venice. It sounded wonderfully romantic. We explored more of Rome for the remainder of the day. That night we explored more of each other. I didn't think that I could ever let him go. I decided not think about that at all. At least not for the next week.

The train ride from Rome to Verona was just under three hours on the high-speed train. The scenery was beautiful as we passed through the Tuscan farmlands. The train was ultra modern and comfortable.

Verona was splendid, and it was easy to see why the city was celebrated by Shakespeare in *Romeo and Juliet*. I thought about the tragic love story of those two star-crossed lovers. Theirs was a forbidden passion because of their feuding families. Not quite the same as my relationship with Matteo, but Shakespeare's tale of tragedy hit home to me in a way that I had not expected.

We approached the famous courtyard of Juliet's house and I was taken at the love notes stuck on the walls and doors at the entrance to the courtyard. Matteo and I looked up at Casa di Giulietta (Juliet's Balcony) where Romeo declared his love for Juliet. I didn't even care that the two were very likely figments of Shakespeare's imagination. It is, after all, probably the most powerful love story in western culture. I was happy to be sharing in some small part of that. Naturally, I hoped for a very different ending for my own love story with Matteo.

I felt Matteo lightly squeeze my hand and then heard his voice. His voice was so very sexy. And it wasn't just his incredible Italian accent. Words had a way of rolling off his tongue and floating through the air to my ears.

I looked into his eyes. They reflected the sunlight, and I was lost in his gaze.

"Amanda? . . . Hello?" he called to me as he waved his hand in front of my face. I gave a slight shake of my head to bring me back from my trance.

"Oh . . . sorry," I said. I guess I was daydreaming.

"The story of Romeo and Juliet can do that," he replied. "Such an amazing, even though tragic, love story."

"They deserved a better ending than they got. So very sad."

"It would not have been a tragedy if they got a better ending," said Matteo.

"That is true. But I like happily ever afters," I said.

"Not everyone gets one," he said with a hint of sadness in his voice.

I let those words swirl around in my head. I was hoping that it was a general observation or one specific to *Romeo and Juliet*. I didn't even want to consider that he could be implying our fate. But I had my doubts, too.

"Do you think that it is possible, even when everything seems stacked against a couple, for them to find happiness together? I mean, could it have been different for Romeo and Juliet?"

"For them? No. I don't think so. It would have changed their story. Then it wouldn't have been *Romeo and Juliet* as we know it. For another couple . . . perhaps it is possible."

"What about for us?" I asked sheepishly.

Matteo turned toward me and took his hands in mine. He looked deep into my eyes. He leaned close.

"I want us to find a way," he spoke softly. Then he leaned in closer and kissed me tenderly on the lips. I fell into his arms and let him hold me. We stayed that way for a while. No one paid us any attention. Another couple who were overcome by the story of *Romeo and Juliet*.

"*I want us to find a way.*" Was not a direct answer to my question. It was probably the best that either of us could offer at the moment. Our future was as uncertain as ever. But we had the here and now. Carpe Diem, I suppose.

We eventually took the tour of Juliet's house. It was owned by the family dell Capello. Probably where Shakespeare came up with Capulet. The house dates from the 13th century. We could see the family coat-of-arms on the wall. I did learn, however, that the balcony itself was added in the 20th century. I guess that doesn't really matter. It certainly didn't seem to faze the young girls who were stepping out onto it to cast their eyes downward to the courtyard hoping to find their Romeo.

We toured the small museum inside the house and made our way back out to the courtyard. Tourists were rubbing the right breast on the bronze sculpture of Juliet for luck. I felt strange doing so, but Matteo had no problem. He smiled widely at me.

"It is for luck," he announced. I giggled.

CHAPTER 25

We enjoyed a lovely lunch and spent most of the afternoon taking in many of Verona's sites. We had reservations on an evening train to Venice. It was just under an hour ride, which gave us time for a lite dinner in the cafe car.

The arrival into Venice was pretty amazing. The train approached through Venice's lagoon in the Adriatic Sea. After we arrived, Matteo led us to his family's apartment. It was located in the San Marco district of Venice directly along the Grand Canal.

The apartment sat on the top floor of the three story building. I was mesmerized by the incredible view of the Grand Canal from the living room. The apartment was spacious with three bedrooms and three bathrooms. It was a dazzling space with a traditional 'altana' roof terrace. Matteo poured us some wine, and we sat out on the terrace and took in the view of the canal. I was living the most romantic day of my life.

"This is absolutely incredible. What a stunning view."

We watched as gondolas and other boats passed on the Grand Canal three floors below.

"This has to be one of the most romantic cities in the world," I announced.

"Si. I have traveled many places. I believe that it is. Especially when you have someone special to share it with."

Matteo reached out and placed his hand on top of mine. His skin was warm. His fingers soothing as he traced them along my hand.

"I am very excited to show you Venice," said Matteo.

"Lead on," I replied.

We began our tour of Venice near the Rialto Bridge with a walk in the footsteps of Casanova along the calle de Spade. Matteo took me into Do Spade for a glass of wine. He informed me that it was where Casanova met his lovers. After, we crossed back over the Rialto Bridge and strolled in and out of shops. I picked up a few souvenirs and sampled pastries.

"Ah, I want to show you something," Matteo said after about twenty minutes more of strolling. "Come with me."

Matteo took me by the hand and led me to a small passageway between two houses. There was a heart carved above the arched entryway.

"This is the Sotoportego dei Preti," he informed me. "Legend has it that if a couple touches the heart together that they will have eternal love."

We reached out our hands together and touched the heart. I didn't know about legends of eternal love, but I was willing to try anything to change the fortunes of our relationship. I could not complain about our getaway to Venice – I would be crazy to do that. Nonetheless, I was still uneasy about what was going to happen to us when my vacation in Italy came to and end.

Fortunately, negative thoughts left my mind as Matteo leaned in and kissed me. He drew me into his arms and held me close as we kissed. Another couple stopped in front of the archway and touched the heart. *Here's to eternal love.*

We ate lunch in a cafe and then headed toward Saint Mark's Square. We visited The Doge's Palace, a marvelous Gothic structure. It was the residence of the Doge, or ruler of Venice, and the headquarters of the Venetian Republic, a city state that existed more than 1,000 years. It now serves as a museum with elaborate exterior and interior architecture, grand halls, and priceless paintings by Venetian masters.

I got my art geek on and thoroughly enjoyed myself. It also didn't hurt that I was on the arm of the sexiest man in Venice. I heard that George Clooney loved Italy. I'm sure he had been to Venice. Even if he were in Venice at that very moment, I would still be more than happy to be with Matteo. Although George and Matteo would make quite a pair on either arm.

I pushed all lustful desires aside as we approached the Basilica San Marco – the Basilica of Saint Mark.

"What do you think Professor Evans?" asked Matteo.

"A superb example of Byzantine architecture dedicated to Venice's patron and the city's main basilica," I answered in my most professorial voice. Actually, I wasn't sure that I had developed my professorial voice yet. But it sounded pretty good to me.

"There are marvelous treasures inside. Byzantine mosaics and painting by leading Venetian artists," added Matteo.

We enjoyed a wonderful tour of the basilica and its art.

"Ora, per la parte più grande di una visita a Venezia (Now, for the grandest part of visiting Venice). At least, in my humble opinion," said Matteo.

We walked five minutes past Saint Mark's Square to the gondola station at Bocino Orseolo. Matteo had reserved a gondola ride for two. We sat close with our arms wrapped around each other. The gondola glided through smaller waterways and then out onto the Grand Canal.

I hadn't realized it before coming to Venice that the Grand Canal is the main street of Venice. There are no cars in Venice. Boats and walking are the main modes of transportation. The

Grand Canal is lined with impressive buildings, formerly homes to all the wealthy families of Venice. I pictured the once highly decorated exteriors with colorful paintings and mosaics. Most have faded to one color, but many still have the ornate, oriental facades influenced by the merchant trading with the East.

Matteo and I shared a kiss as we passed under a bridge. I ran my hand across the stubble on his face. The five o'clock shadow adding to his sex appeal. I traced my fingers around his chin and up to his lips. He kissed my finger with a smile.

"I wish we could just stay here in Venice," I said.

"If only all wishes could come true."

"There has to be a way," I said.

"To stay in Venice?" asked Matteo.

"No. Well, yes, that would be incredible, but probably not realistic. I'm hoping that we can truly find a way to make it work between us. I can't imagine my life without you in it."

"Please, Amanda, let's not speak of this now. I just want to enjoy being together. We will figure it all out. I promise."

"I am going to hold you to that promise."

He gently ran his hand across my cheek. "Così molto bello. So very beautiful."

CHAPTER 26

We had reservations for dinner at Ristorante Quadri. Matteo suggested that I get ready in the en-suite master bathroom while he used one of the guest bathrooms. Quadri was an elegant restaurant, so I picked a black dress. That was the great thing about a black dress, it presented as formal even when it was sexy.

I was wearing a Slate & Willow Blaire dress. It was meant to catch Matteo's eye with its flattering style. I was going for a little daring and a little sweet. This was the perfect dress for that. It was black and sleeveless. It was a full skirt with an above the knee hemline.

I selected black high-heel shoes. I wasn't totally convinced that I could navigate a cobblestone street, but all the more reason to hang on to Matteo's arm. Not that I needed an additional reason.

Matteo wandered into my bedroom as I was searching through my luggage for the perfect accessories to match the dress.

"Tu sei la donna più bella che io abbia mai visto. (*You are the most gorgeous woman that I have ever seen*)," he said as he entered the bedroom.

My Italian wasn't perfect, but I certainly got the gist of what he was saying. I smiled. I turned toward him. He was dressed in a charcoal, slim-cut suit. He had on a crisp white shirt and sable solid slim tie.

"Thank you for the comment," I said. "Now, let me try. ou sono l'uomo più bello che abbia mai visto (*You are the most handsome man I have ever seen*)."

"Grazie," Matteo said with a modest grin.

I held up a kate spade cobblestone bib necklace. The black and gold cobblestones a perfect match with my dress. "Can you help me put this on?" I asked.

Matteo walked over. I handed him the necklace and turned around. He draped the necklace over my upper chest and clasped it around the back of my neck. Then he gently kissed my neck.

I grabbed my clutch in cross-grain black leather and headed toward the door. I could sense Matteo's eyes on me. The dress was doing its job - *A little daring and a little sweet*. I paused in the doorway and turned my head over my shoulder. I offered my best 'come hither' glance.

I moved through the doorway. I heard Matteo's footsteps across the floor. He caught up to me and took me by the hand.

It was a relatively short walk to the restaurant. I managed in my shoes just fine. That, however, did not deter me from looping my arm through Matteo's and holding tight.

Ristorante Quadri is a Michelin starred restaurant located in Saint Mark's Square. It has one of Venice's most incredible views as it looks out over the square. The atmosphere in the dining room was both elegant and relaxed. It afforded us to take full advantage of the charming view of Saint Mark's Square just beyond the windows.

"The menu is a contemporary interpretation of traditional Venetian and Italian dishes," said Matteo.

I ordered the Burrata cheese ravioli with seafood stew, tomatoes and oregano. Matteo had the Fried langoustine rolls with cod bottarga and almond sauce. We paired our meals with a wonderful selection of wine. The food was marvelous as the flavors danced on my taste buds.

Piazza San Marco was an amazing view, but I was most interested in the view across the table. Matteo looked every bit like the leading man in a romantic movie. I couldn't imagine a more perfect dinner date. Well, I guess that wasn't completely true.

What would make it more perfect would include knowing Matteo and I did have an eternal love. That this would be one of many dinner dates we should share. I was desperately going for a carpe diem approach to our time together. I just didn't want it to end.

We finished dinner and split a chocolate souffle for dessert. We took a late night stroll through St. Mark's Square toward the apartment. There were few tourists or locals at this hour. The square was also absent of the many pigeons that frequent the grounds during the day.

The stunning architecture surrounded us. Light from the streetlamps suffused the square and cast beautiful shadows and patterns. Moonbeams created a bit of back light and glistened off the water of the lagoon. I rested my head against Matteo as we walked.

"It is so peaceful this time of night," I commented.

"Like our own private piazza," added Matteo.

We could see distant lights on the balconies and rooftop terraces as Venetians, tourists, and other visitors to the city enjoyed the summer evening. We made the most of Venice before it was time to return to Rome.

I cried for most of the train ride back, I cried myself to sleep my final night in Italy, and I cried at the airport as Matteo and I said goodbye.

"No," Matteo said as he gently lifted my chin with his hand. "This is not goodbye. We will see each other again."

I wanted to believe him. I wanted to believe we could find a way for Matteo to move to California. But I knew it wasn't a simple matter. Yes, he could visit. A work visa was an entirely different matter.

Maybe Jenny could help find Matteo something at Pacific Coast Pictures. It wouldn't be easy. She had already told me it was nearly impossible to get the studio to sponsor a visa unless the foreign filmmaker was a "must have" for the studio.

Through tears, Matteo and I shared a tender kiss and a final hug before I needed to make my way through the airport gauntlet. We had plans for him to visit over my Thanksgiving break, but it seemed so far away. And would that only make it more difficult if we couldn't find a way for him to move? I pushed it all out of my mind as grabbed my luggage and got in line at the security checkpoint.

I made my way through security at the airport and was gathering all my items from the plastic bin while simultaneously slipping my feet into my shoes. I was moving as quickly as I could, but the flow of passengers through the security screening kept coming and I was feeling rushed.

Most other passengers were going through a similar ritual to me in gathering their belongings. A few had packed more efficiently than I had and simply grabbed their one or two items and moved around me.

I shoved my boarding pass back into my carry-on bag and double checked that I had everything. I moved on from the security checkpoint and into the sprawling terminal. People moved in all directions with no clear traffic pattern. Some passengers were speed walking from gate to gate for connecting flights. One man was running as the final boarding call was announced for a flight several gates away.

I still had nearly two hours before my flight boarded. My parents had always drummed into me that if you were early you were never late. I know plenty of people who always arrive just on time. Jenny is definitely one of those people. But I guess I had spent my entire life arriving early for everything. I also had never been late. On more than a few occasions I arrived on time only because I had left early.

I located my gate. Most of the waiting area was full with passengers waiting for the flight that was departing before mine. I decided to check out the selection of restaurants in the terminal. I was a little hungry and it would help pass the time. I found one that I looked good. I found a table and ordered. I thought of Matteo as I waited for my food.

We had shared a long and passionate kiss goodbye when he dropped me off. We promised that it wasn't the end for us. We still didn't know how we were going to make it work, but neither of us was ready to be the one to say it was over. We had spent a magical week in Venice. He made me breakfast this morning before driving me to the airport.

I wanted to just enjoy the memory of our kiss, but the reality of navigating the airport for an international flight took over as soon as I entered the airport. Now, sitting by myself at a table, with plenty of time before my flight, all I could think of was Matteo. This should be playing out so differently.

I finished my lunch and headed toward my gate. I had an hour before my flight and figured I should be able to find a seat in the gate's waiting area. I plopped down in an empty seat and pulled my kindle out of my carry-on bag. I was looking forward to getting lost in the romance book from one of my favorite authors. Before I even had a chance to turn on my kindle, my cell phone rang.

My parents were calling. I answered to my mother's distraught voice.

"Are you still in Rome?" she asked me.

"I'm at the airport. I'm waiting for my flight," I answered. "What's wrong?"

"It's Tina. She's in the hospital. You should come home and be with the family."

"What happened?"

"Some sort of overdose . . ." my mother started crying.

"Mom, it will be okay. I'm booked on a connecting flight from New York to Los Angeles. I will just get a flight from New York to Boston."

"Okay," my mother managed to get out between crying.

"I will call Scott or Holly with details and to pick me up at Logan," I said.

"Okay," my mother said again.

"Mom, I'm sure everything will be alright." I wasn't sure at all. I had no idea what Tina had overdosed on or what her condition was. It was all that I could think to say. At least it was what my Mom needed to hear at that moment.

"Mom, I need to go so that I can change my flight out of New York. I love you."

"I love you too, sweetheart. Have a safe flight."

I could still hear my mother crying as she hung up the phone. We had years of Tina's drama. But it had never been this bad. Whatever happened, Tina had taken a dangerous turn in life. She and I didn't see eye to eye on anything. Tina brought all her trouble on herself. But none of that was important right now. My only concern was that she was going to get better.

I approached the airline counter at the gate. A cheerful woman greeted me in Italian. I replied in my best Italian. She quickly switched to English with a warm smile.

"I need to make a change to my ticket out of New York," I told her.

She asked for my name and to see identification. I told her as I pulled my Passport out of my bag and handed it to her. She was already typing away on her keyboard and intently looking at the screen. She glanced down at my passport to confirm my name.

"Yes. I see that you are on the 7:30 flight out of New York's JFK to Los Angeles. What change do you wish to make?"

"I need to change my flight to Boston."

"Let me see what is available." She tapped away more at her keyboard and watched the screen. There was a reflection on the lenses of her glasses of flight information from the computer screen. "There are a few seats left on an 8:00 flight from JFK to Boston."

"That would be fine," I said.

"Okay, let's see about making that change." She typed away some more. "There will be a $100 change fee."

Because it was a same day booking, my flight from New York to Boston was going to cost about the same as the flight from New York to LA. So I had no real credit to speak of once that was factored in. When I added in the $100 change fee, it was going to cost me slightly more to fly the 185 miles to Boston than it would have the 2,475 miles to Los Angeles. At least most of it was already covered. Of course I would still need to book a Boston to LA flight at some point.

None of that mattered right now. All I could think of was my little sister. *What did you do to yourself Tina?*

The airline gate attendant printed off my boarding pass for the flight from JFK to Logan. I went and sat back down. I called my brother Scott.

"Mom told me that you might be calling," Scott said when he answered the phone.

"Mom didn't tell me much. What happened?" I said.

"Tina hooked up with her latest boyfriend and tried cocaine. The shock to her system nearly killed her."

"Oh, stuff!"

"Fortunately, someone had the good sense to call an ambulance right away. They were able to save her, but she's in ICU at Mass General Hospital."

"My flight is scheduled to arrive at 9:15 tonight. Can either you or Holly pick me up at Logan?"

"I will pick you up. Holly wants to stay with Mom and Dad."

"Mom was crying when she called me," I said.

"She's been doing a lot of that. Dad is being strong, but I have never seen him look so worried. They thought that they had that creep out of Tina's life. She even seemed to be doing okay at the job that Dad got for her in his office . . ." Scott's voice trailed off.

"What are the doctors saying?" I asked. I needed to know what I would be walking into when I got to Boston.

"Not much right now. She's stable but not out of the woods yet."

"I'll see you tonight."

"Later. Have a safe trip."

We ended our call, and I tossed my phone into my bag. I sat back in my seat and stared at the ceiling. My day had gone from bad to worse. I still had sixteen hours ahead of me before Scott would pick me up from the airport. It was going to be an extremely long trip. And I doubted that I would be able to sleep for any of it. I could feel tears forming in my eyes.

An elderly woman next to me handed me a tissue. I thanked her and wiped my eyes. The subtle kindness of a stranger. I would take whatever I could get at that point. I said a prayer for Tina. Forty minutes later I boarded the plane and settled into my seat for the trans-Atlantic flight.

CHAPTER 27

Nearly seventeen hours later, I got into Scott's car outside of Terminal C at Logan airport. We shared a quick hug. A Logan Express bus and a hotel shuttle van passed. Then Scott pulled into the flow of traffic exiting the airport.

"How is Tina?" I asked once we were moving steadily.

"About the same," he replied.

"And how are Mom and Dad holding up?"

"They are doing a little better. Holly and I finally convinced them to go back to the house for the evening. It wasn't doing them any good just staring at her in the hospital bed. Holly even tried to fix them some dinner, but they weren't very hungry."

"What, exactly, happened? What was Tina doing trying hard drugs?"

Scott shook his head. He seemed at a complete loss to understand how far Tina had spiraled out of control. This was foreign to all of us, but especially Scott. He was the most straight laced of any of us. He was an Academic All American in high school and took every AP class available. He aced everything. He graduated top of his class in college and had graduate programs competing for him. Scott had been a professor at Boston College for five years and was a star in their Economics department.

"Do you think she will be alright?" I finally asked to break the silence.

"That's a bit relative at the moment. Will she survive? Yes. Will she physically recover? I think there is a good chance of that. But I don't know if she will be 'alright.' Amanda, she needs a lot of help. More help than any of us realized. I feel bad."

"I fell bad, too. We all do."

"No. I mean that I feel bad that I didn't notice more of what was going on. I'm sure there were signs that something like this was going to happen," he replied.

We were on the Mass Pike heading toward my parents' house in Cambridge. We passed Fenway Park. The lights were on for a night game. It was only then that I realized Scott had the game on the radio. It was more background noise. Scott loved the Red Sox. The one thing that he splurged on was a partial season ticket package. I was willing to bet that even he didn't know what the score of that night's game was.

"Scott, you can't blame yourself. None of us can. Tina has always surrounded herself with drama. Always of her own making. But I don't think that any of us could have envisioned her doing anything this extreme."

"I should have done more to keep her away from that loser she's been dating. He was really bad news."

"Same guy that got busted a few weeks ago and Tina wanted bail money for?"

"That's the guy," Scott replied. "Dad even helped get him into a good rehab program. Tina promised she would stay away from him. She was liking her job in Dad's office. She had moved back in with Mom and Dad until she got her stuff straightened out. Everything seemed to be going okay. We were cautiously optimistic. Then . . . next thing we know, Mom and Dad get a call from the police that Tina is being rushed to Mass General Hospital."

"What about what's his name?"

"He took off before the ambulance and police arrived. But the cops knew exactly who he was. They picked him up for questioning yesterday. Haven't gotten much out of him yet. He was stoned out of his mind."

"He'll probably deny even being with her," I said.

"A lot of witnesses. One girl said that he was the one who brought the drugs to the party and convinced Tina try them. Off course he got her good and drunk first. Mom and Dad thought Tina was at dinner with a friend she had made in the office. They feel terrible. They think they should have insisted she stay home."

"They can't blame themselves. My goodness, they have done so much for her. For all of us. They raised her to make better decisions. She's an adult. She's responsible for the bad decisions in her life. I just hope you are right that she will fully recover from this one."

"We've already looked into rehab for her. A place in New Hampshire. Far away from everything. Just a place to get clean and figure out how to move forward."

"Let me know what I can do. Visiting Tina, helping to pay for it . . . whatever is needed. Tina has always been a pain in the ass, but she is our sister. I love her. I want her to have a good life."

"We all do. We'll figure it out."

We were on Memorial Drive and crossed over the Charles River. The river was to our left and the John F. Kennedy School of Government at Harvard University was on our right. We rounded the bend and headed for Brattle Street. A few more turns onto side streets off of Brattle and then we arrived at my parents. They lived in the same Victorian house that we had grown up in.

Scott pulled into the long, narrow driveway behind Holly's car. My dad's car was in front of her's. Mom's car was probably in the garage. She rarely drove. The great thing about where they lived in Cambridge, she could either walk or take the subway pretty much everywhere she needed to go.

I hadn't been home for a visit in nearly a year. I wished that I was visiting under better circumstances. Dad had the Red Sox game on the television. Both my parents got up from the couch when we entered the living room. I hugged them both.

"What's the score?" Scott asked our dad. Trying to gain some sense of normalcy.

"I think the Sox are up by two," my dad replied. "I'm not really sure. I haven't been paying very close attention."

Scott nodded his head that he knew exactly.

"Where's Holly?" I asked.

"She's taking a shower," answered my Mom. Her eyes were puffy and red. I guessed that she only stopped crying very recently. Maybe as soon as just before we entered the house.

"Can we get you two anything?" I asked my parents.

"No. Thank you, honey," Dad replied. Mom shook her head no.

"I'm just going to freshen up," I said.

"Oh, of course, dear," said my mom. "You must be exhausted after traveling for so long."

"I'll be okay. The jet lag will probably hit me tomorrow."

"Why don't you take a shower to relax," added my mother. "Holly is in your kids' bathroom, but you can either use ours or the bathroom on the third floor."

My parents still referred to our rooms and bathroom as our kids'. I guess that was pretty typical for parents. No matter how long you have been an adult, you are always your parents' children.

"Let me help you with your luggage," offered Scott.

"Thanks." I flashed him a quick sisterly smile. He picked up my large suitcase and carried it up the stairs.

"I'll be down in a bit," I told my parents.

I grabbed my carry-on bag and followed Scott up the stairs. Scott placed my suitcase in my old bedroom. It looked exactly the same as the day that I moved out after high school. I spent school vacations in the room during college, but hadn't spent more than a week at a time in the house since I had started graduate school.

"Mom and Dad don't change a thing," said Scott with a smile.

"Maybe someday they will," I said.

"They told me that they will update our rooms for grandchildren to visit," said Scott. "Their subtle way of suggesting that we all should get married and have children."

"Oh, so they are actually subtle with you?" I said. "The day I earned my doctorate they wanted to know if Brad and I had discussed getting married yet."

"They must have been crushed when you told them that you two were breaking up."

"That would be an understatement," I said.

"Hey you two." I turned as Holly walked into my room. We hugged.

"It is so good to see you," she said to me. Her hair was still damp from the shower. She was wearing a pair of Old Navy pajama shorts with a matching tank top.

Holly was younger than me, but we had been the same size since junior high school. It was great because we often borrowed each others clothes. It also stunk, because Holly would often borrow my clothes without asking.

She had similar blond hair and brown eyes to me. We actually looked a lot alike. Anyone could tell we were sisters. Many people confused us growing up.

"How were your flights?" Holly asked me.

"Long. But otherwise they were fine. I'm going to take a quick shower."

"See you downstairs. I'm going to check on Mom and Dad," said Holly. She looked at Scott. "Are you staying tonight too?"

"I think so. But it will be strange to sleep in my old bedroom," he replied.

"Just don't crank up your Green Day CDs," said Holly.

"As long as I don't hear any Mariah Cary coming from your room," Scott said to Holly.

Holly and Scott always went at it over music. That both Green Day and Mariah Carry had top songs ten years ago was about all that the two shared in common when it came to music.

"I'm going to take my shower now," I said. I padded off toward the bathroom. A shower would feel good. As much as I hated the reason why we were all back in the house, it was nice to be here with my family. I even missed Tina raising hell. Oh how I wanted her to get better.

I showered and wrapped a towel around me and headed toward my bedroom.

"Mom. What are you doing?" My mother was pulling clothes out of my suitcase.

"I'm doing a load of laundry," she said.

"It's after ten o'clock. That can wait. And I can do my own laundry."

"Nonsense." My mother eased past me with the laundry basket in her hands.

"Don't waste your breath," called Holly from her room.

She was right. If Mom insisted on doing laundry, then there was no convincing her otherwise. Besides, it probably helped take her mind off of Tina. Holly stepped into the hallway.

"Here," she said as she handed me a pair of pajamas. "I brought a couple of pairs. I figured that most of your stuff might be dirty after two weeks in Italy."

"Thanks," I said as I took the panties, shorts and shirt from her. "A small payback for all the times you borrowed my clothes."

"Hey, you borrowed mine as well."

"Not nearly as often as you did mine. And I always asked first." Then I smiled. Holly and I were very close. I missed not living nearby and being able to see her often.

"You look beat. Why don't you try to get some sleep," she said to me.

"I think I will."

I said good night to Holly, Scott, and my parents and turned in. I was actually fading fast and wouldn't have been much company. I had sent Matteo a text message before I boarded the plane in Rome and told him what was going on. I told him that I would get in touch tomorrow. It was already tomorrow in Rome, but just 4:30 in the morning. I would wait and text Matteo when I got up.

I crawled under the covers and don't even remember my head hitting the pillow. I dreamed about my family. I also dreamed about Matteo. There was a lot going on in my life at the moment. I remember in my dream state being glad that I still had nearly a month before I started teaching at UCLA. Maybe by then everything would be better.

CHAPTER 28

We had good news when we arrived at the hospital. They were moving Tina out of ICU and into a regular room. The doctor told us that Tina was now alert and that we could visit her just as soon as they had her settled into her new room.

"When will she be able to go home?" my mom asked the doctor.

"We'd like to keep her a few more days. We are also coordinating with the rehabilitation facility in hopes that you will be able to bring her directly to the program after she is discharged."

We thanked the doctor and then went for some coffee while we waited to see Tina. A nurse had told us that it would probably be about thirty minutes.

"How are you doing, Mom?" I asked.

"Knowing that Tina is out of ICU is a huge relief. I am just praying that she can get the proper help."

"White Mountains Clinic has an excellent program. One of the best in New England," offered Scott. "I hear they can work small miracles."

"Scott is right, dear. Tina will get the help she needs there," added my dad. "They also have resources for the family to make sure that we are supported and know how best to support Tina when she finishes the program."

"Everything is going to work out," added Holly.

Twenty minutes later we headed upstairs. We stopped by the nurses station and were informed that Tina was settled into her new room and that we could visit. When we walked into the room she turned and looked at us. I think she was uncertain of how to react. Mostly because she was not sure how we were going to react.

My mom and dad went directly to her and gave her a huge hug and kiss. Tina's face seemed to soften then. Maybe she knew that things were going to be okay.

"The doctors say that I am lucky," were the first words out of Tina's mouth. She spoke before Scott, Holly, or myself had a chance to say anything. "They tell me that I almost died."

My mom had tears in her eyes again. "Sweetie, let's not talk about that right now. You are going to be okay."

"No. I need to talk about it. I really messed up this time. This is way bigger than getting fired from a job or dating some deadbeat loser." Tina was looking straight ahead. No eye contact and little emotion. She was concentrating on what she was saying.

"We are going to get you the help that you need," said my dad.

"Tina, we found a great program in New Hampshire. The White Mountain Clinic," said Scott.

"They will take great care of you there," added Holly. "And we're here for you."

"All of us are here for you. We love you, little sister," I said.

Tina broke down and started crying. "I'm sorry," she sobbed. "I'm so sorry."

My parents were on either side of Tina's bed. They rested their heads against hers. Scott and Holly Sat on the end of the bed on one side and I sat on the other. We spent quite some time like that. We wanted Tina to know that her family loved her and that we were going to get her through this.

After a while, Tina seemed to be in better spirits. She even began to talk about how she wanted to go to Cape Cod after she finished her rehab program. We took a family vacation to the Cape every summer when we were growing up. Those were some of our fondest memories of childhood.

Then Tina turned toward me. She was still a bit pale, but I figured she must look much better than she had yesterday. She even had a slight grin on her face.

"Are you going to see Brad while you are here?" Tina asked me.

"I . . . I don't know. I hadn't even thought of it. I wasn't even planning on being here - -"

"Until what happened to me," Tina said.

"Yes. But, Tina, I want to be here. You're my baby sister. I love you," I replied.

"Even though I am a pain in the ass?"

"That's part of being the little sister."

"You didn't really answer Tina's question," said Holly.

"What?" I asked.

"About Brad. Are you going to see him while you are here?"

"I said that I don't know. That is an answer."

"It would be wonderful to see Bradley," offered my mom.

"Would be something if he makes the Patriots," said my dad.

"Okay, enough about Brad," I said. "He and I broke up. I am here to visit Tina. I don't see—"

"I think you should see him," said Tina.

My family and I went back and forth like that for a few minutes until they finally dropped it. I honestly hadn't thought about it until Tina brought it up. I knew that Brad was in the area preparing for the New England Patriots training camp. They had drafted him as a top prospect. But this was an unscheduled visit on my part. I had been focused on Tina.

A nurse came in and suggested that Tina get some rest. We all gave my sister a hug and kiss goodbye and told her we would be by the next day for another visit. I was the last to reach the door.

"Thanks for coming," Tina said to me just before I exited her room. I turned toward her. She was smiling and had a warm glow in her eyes that I hadn't seen in a long time.

"You keep getting better. Luv ya," I said.

"I will. Luv ya, too."

I nodded and then joined my parents, Scott, and Holly in the hallway. We were all relieved that Tina had turned an important corner. We decided to go out to lunch. I wish that my visit were under happier circumstances, but it was nice spending time with my family. Plus, things were definitely looking up for Tina. For the first time in a long time, I had a good feeling about where Tina was headed with her life.

We were riding the T's Red Line train back to Cambridge. Scott and my dad were talking about sports. Holly and my mom were talking about education. Both my mom and Holly were school teachers. I was happy to zone out a little.

I realized that my cell phone was buzzing in my purse. I dug it out and saw that it was Matteo calling. I answered.

"Hi. It must be the middle of the night there," I said.

"Yes. It is very late. But I needed to speak with you." His voice was somber and stressed

"I don't like the sounds of this," I replied.

"I have been doing some research," Matteo said. "There is no way I am getting a work visa. If I wasn't good enough to win the internship and scholarship, how could I be good enough for a movie studio to want to sponsor a work visa for me?"

"What about applying for some film courses at USC? Then you could get a student visa. Then Jenny could help get you in at Pacific Coast Pictures. Who knows, after that you could try—"

Matteo interjected. "Amanda, it is not realistic. I've been living with my head in the clouds. I am going to work with my family at the winery. It is best."

"What about making movies?"

"A silly dream. I can work on them part-time. As a hobby. I am a Rosetti. We are winemakers. Not filmmakers."

"Matteo, I don't understand. This is all so sudden."

"Amanda, I don't see any way we can have a relationship living 6,300 miles apart. And I am coming to terms with the reality that I am not going to get to California to make movies."

"Matteo, there has to be a way. Let me talk to Jenny. Let me talk to the USC film department . . ." my voice trailed off. My eyes moistened.

"I'm sorry, Amanda. It is easier for both of us if we face reality and move on with our lives." Matteo's voice broke with sadness. "I wish things could be different."

I was trying to hold back my tears. The last thing I wanted to do was start balling my eyes out on the subway. We were silent for a beat. Then Matteo spoke softly. "I will treasure what we had with all my heart."

"Me, too," were the only words I could manage to sepak.

"Lei è una bella persona (*You are a beautiful person*)," said Matteo. Then he ended our call. Neither one of us wanted to say 'goodbye' or 'I will miss you.' Those seemed to final. But it was hard to see any realistic future for us now. It sure seemed like goodbye.

CHAPTER 29

I managed to keep it together, but I felt terrible for the rest of the day. Jet lag also set in. That actually gave me an excuse to turn in early. I curled up under the covers and had a good long cry. It was eerily reminiscent of my teenage years when my first love broke up with me. I survived that. I figured I would survive this.

After I cried myself out and tossed and turned for an hour, pure exhaustion took over. I don't remember falling asleep. But I slept hard and for a long time. The next thing I knew is that I rolled over and sunlight was streaming into my room.

I could smell bacon and eggs. I rolled out of bed and stretched. It was already after nine. I slept a solid eleven hours. I felt pretty good. I crossed the room and opened my bedroom door. I could hear laughter from the kitchen. I was groggy and a little disoriented. *Am I dreaming?*

"Hey, come downstairs," said Scott as he darted out of the bathroom and flicked me on the arm. It didn't hurt, but I could still feel where Scott had flicked me. He did that all that time when we were kids. Okay, definitely not dreaming.

I padded down the stairs. The carpet runner was plush under my feet. The wood floor at the bottom of the stairs was cooler and hard. I turned in the foyer and headed down the hall to the kitchen.

"Wonderful news," said my mother as I stepped into the kitchen. "The hospital called. Tina is making even more improvement. She will be discharged tomorrow, and the clinic has a spot ready for her in the program."

"That is wonderful news," I said.

"Sit down, breakfast is almost ready," said Holly.

"It smells great," I said. I poured myself a cup of coffee.

The front doorbell rang. My mother jumped out of her seat. "I'll get it," she said.

"I can get it, Mom," said Scott.

"Sit. I've got it," she said to him.

"Woof," replied Scott as he sat back down.

"Don't be a wise guy," Mom said to him.

Scott was about to say something about how hard it was not to be a wise guy when you have a PhD, but he let it go. Besides, my mother was already halfway to the front door.

"She expecting the Publisher's Clearing House Prize Patrol," I said. I was only half joking. I remember my mother always filling out the entries in hopes of winning millions of dollars. She had never won, but we always had subscriptions to *People* magazine.

"I'm so glad you could make it," I heard my mother say to whoever was at the front door.

"Mom invited someone to breakfast?" I asked.

"I guess so," replied Scott. He took a sip of his coffee. Holly scooped eggs into a serving dish. Dad piled crisp pieces of turkey bacon onto a plate.

"Let me help," I insisted. I got up and grabbed the plate of toast off the counter.

"Look who's here," announced Mom. I turned and nearly dropped the plate. Dad took the plate of toast from me.

"Hi everybody," said my ex-boyfriend, Brad. I suddenly felt very self-conscious. I was still wearing Holly's borrowed pajama shorts and t-shirt top. I hadn't even checked myself in the mirror, but I'm sure I had bed head. I quickly cupped my hand in front of my mouth and exhaled. Yep, morning breath. What is my mother up to?

"Brad, what are you doing here?" I asked.

"Amanda Rose Evans, is that any way to greet our guest?" said my mother.

"I never knew that your middle name was Rose," said Brad.

I nodded slightly. "It was my grandmother's name. I'm sorry, it's nice to see you. It's just that I didn't know you were coming." I flashed a look at my mother.

She just shrugged her shoulders and smiled. *Mom! What are you doing?*

"I should go upstairs and change," I announced. "Excuse me."

What is wrong with me? Why does any of this even matter? I was caught off guard that is all. It flustered me. I don't think straight when I am flustered. I was in my panties and looking for a bra in the pile of clean clothes my mother had left on a chair.

"What was that all about?" Holly asked me.

"Don't you knock?" I asked. Holly ignored my question and closed the door behind her.

I dressed in a crew t-shirt and a pair of chino shorts. I sat on the bed and put on a pair of ankle socks and sneakers. I stepped in front of the mirror and combed out my hair.

"Okay," said Holly, "back to my original question. What was that downstairs?"

"I don't know. Mom is up to something."

"Yeah she is. She is trying to get you and Brad back together."

"No kidding, Sherlock."

"Don't be a hater. I'm more wondering about your reaction. You seemed more than a little uncomfortable. I thought you and Brad mutually ended your relationship on good terms."

"We did," I answered. "On great terms, actually."

"So what is the big deal? You still carrying a torch for him?"

"No. We were never that serious."

"Sure you weren't."

"Holly, we both knew it wasn't going to last beyond his graduating from USC. We were always headed in different directions."

"But you enjoyed being with him?"

"Sure. What wasn't to enjoy. He's handsome, smart, caring, and fun."

"So what was missing?"

"I don't know. We never planned on more. So, I guess, we never looked for more."

I finished combing out my hair. "How's it look?" I asked.

"Fine. But why do you care? I mean, you're not trying to impress anyone . . . are you?"

"No. Of course not. But I don't want to look like a slob that just rolled out of bed. I wouldn't go out in public the way I had looked."

"Uh huh. There is something else. What gives?"

"Do you promise not to say anything?" I asked.

"Of course."

"There was this guy in Italy."

"What?! A guy in Italy?"

"Girls, are you almost ready?!" My mother called from the bottom of the stairs.

"Just a minute!" Holly called back. "Okay, give me the Reader's Digest version."

"His name is Matteo. We met just after I finished teaching my course in Rome. Holly, he is so incredibly handsome and wonderful. I was drawn to him the instant we met. He felt the same way. Long story short, we made a real connection. We spent a week together at his family's place in Venice."

"Amanda! Wow, that is not like you."

"I know. It surprised me, too. But it felt so right."

"So what are you going to do?"

"I don't think anything, now. He called me yesterday. He is staying in Italy. It's over."

"Amanda, I know you must feel bad. But how long did you know this guy? What, two weeks? You had a whirlwind romance in Italy with him. I'd say that constitutes a pretty incredible vacation. Chalk it up to a nice experience, with some great memories, and move on."

"You're probably right. In my head that is what I keep telling myself. But my heart still wants to be with him."

"Do you realistically see that happening?" asked Holly.

"Girls! Breakfast is getting cold!" my mother called from the bottom of the stairs.

I popped a breath mint into my mouth. *Morning breath be gone.* "We better get downstairs," I said.

CHAPTER 30

"Sorry it took us so long," I said when Holly and arrived at the dining room table.

"Amanda you sit between your father and Brad. Holly, sit next to me."

My mother's not-so-subtle seating arrangement.

"What were you girls talking about up there?" Mom asked.

"Nothing much," replied Holly.

"We were just catching up. Girl talk," I said. I picked up the bowl of eggs and passed them to my dad. "Let's eat."

The food passed around the table. Once everyone's plates were full, my father looked over at Brad.

"So, son, how are your workouts going?" he asked Brad.

"Very well, sir. I hired a receivers coach to work me out prior to the start of training camp. I want to be sharp from the very first day."

"The Boston Globe and NESN say the Pats would be crazy not to give you a spot on the roster," my dad said.

"I'm just focused on working my hardest to make the team. It's all I can do," replied Brad.

"I hope you do make the team," said Scott.

"That would be a dream come true. I still can't believe the Patriots drafted me. If I do make the team, I will be sure to get tickets so you can all come to a game. Amanda, maybe you could even fly back."

Scott saved me from having to answer right away. Not that I think that was his intent.

"Maybe we could meet the rest of the team," he said.

"Now just cool it," said my dad. "Brad was nice enough to offer tickets to a game if he makes the team. Don't go pushing his generous offer."

"It's fine, Mr. Evans," said Brad. "If I make the team, of course."

Brad then turned toward me. "Your parents were telling me you were in Italy. You taught a summer course there. How did that go?"

I knew that Brad was genuinely interested in my academic career. Even though he teased me about being a nerd, he was always very supportive of my studies, my research, and my dream to teach Classics at a major university. I told him all about teaching at the American Academy in Rome Classical Summer School. My family listened intently as well. It was the first real chance we had to talk since my trip to Italy.

"And you stayed for some vacation after? Did you get to see all the sights?" Brad asked.

"Yes, I got to be a total classics nerd," I said. I told him everything that I had seen. I left out any reference to Matteo. Even as a friend. Only Holly knew. I planned on keeping it that way. Did that tell me something? Perhaps. I didn't dwell on it. I was being peppered with questions from my family and Brad about Italy.

After breakfast, Brad thanked my parents for inviting him. My mother told me that we were going to visit Holly in a few hours, but she suggested Brad and I take a walk to Harvard Square while they cleaned up. *Jeez, Mom! Why don't you just suggest that we sit on the back porch swing and make out?*

Not an abhorrent thought by any stretch, but my feelings for Matteo were still raw. I didn't need to have not-so-old feelings for Brad getting stirred up right now. Even if he looked better than ever. Even if I could remember what a great kisser he was.

Darn-it Mom! That is exactly what you want me to be thinking.

"Do you even have the time?" I asked Brad.

"Sure. I haven't been to Harvard Square yet. Maybe you can show me where I can pahk my cah in the Havahd Yahd," he said.

"Don't ever do that again," I said.

"Yeah, really, dude. That was a pretty bad impression," said Scott.

"Sorry," said Brad with a grin. He did have a warm and gentle smile.

"Okay. Maybe just a quick walk," I said.

Brad and I headed out the front door. We cut over to Brattle Street. We turned and headed toward Harvard Square.

"I'm sorry if this is awkward for you," Brad said.

"No. It's okay. I am the one who should be apologizing. I don't know what my mother was thinking."

"She's thinking we should could get back together."

"I think that is pretty clear. But she believes what she wants to about the depth of our relationship, not what it was in reality."

"Just because we never made plans to live happily ever after," said Brad, "doesn't mean that I didn't love you."

"I know. I loved you, too. But we never even considered the type of 'I love you' that would have had us walking down the aisle and saying 'I do.'"

"Maybe not."

I stopped on the sidewalk and turned toward Brad. "What do you mean by 'maybe not'?" I asked.

"Nothing. Never mind."

"No. Tell me."

"Look, it's not like I ever considered proposing or anything like that, but I didn't rule that possibility out either . . . not until you made it really clear your future plans didn't include me."

"Whoa, hold on a second," I said as I held up my hand. "I never explicitly said anything like that."

"You didn't have to. All you talked about was getting a university teaching position after you finished your PhD and how I would probably be going on to the NFL somewhere. You never talked about whether those could ever be in the same city. Or if there would be a way to make it work."

"Because that was the most likely scenario. It is what actually happened. I was being realistic. Besides, I never thought you wanted anything more than what we had at USC."

"Fair enough. Maybe I didn't think that I did at the time. I didn't realize how much I would miss you."

"So what are you saying?" I asked.

"Amanda, I don't know. I miss you. I miss being with you. When your mom called and invited me to breakfast, I figured you knew about it and wanted to see me. Maybe you missed me, too."

"Oh, Brad. I am happy to see you. I'm glad that you came over for breakfast. But I didn't know. This was all my mother's doing. I just don't see how this changes anything. I'm in Los Angeles and you are here in Massachusetts."

"Just during football season. The off-season covers the spring semester and most of the summer. We would only really be apart for the fall semester. And I could fly you to some of the games."

"You have actually given this some thought. Haven't you?"

"Amanda, we were good together. It could be even better now if we really wanted to build a life together."

"Brad, I'd be lying if I said that I still didn't have feelings for you. Yes, we were good together. I have no regrets about being with you. None at all. And, even though it was mutual, it was sad when we broke up—"

"We made that decision at the time. We can make a different one now."

Yes, I heard what I was saying. I was willing to start a relationship with Matteo on the hopes he could come to California. But I was not willing to consider a bi-coastal relationship with Brad. My decisions with Brad were rooted in what seemed most practical. My decisions with Matteo more rooted in my feelings.

"I have a lot going on right now, Brad. This isn't the best time for me to be making any major decisions."

"Amanda, I still love you."

CHAPTER 31

I wandered rather aimlessly through Harvard Square. I walked along John F. Kennedy Street, past the John F. Kennedy School of Government and John F. Kennedy Park. The nation's 35th president figured prominently here. I crossed Memorial Drive and took the Anderson Memorial Bridge over the Charles River.

The river separated Cambridge and Boston. When I reached the Boston side of the river, John F. Kennedy Street became North Harvard Street. I crossed over Soldiers Field Road. I walked a little ways down North Harvard Street. The Harvard Business School was on my left and Harvard Stadium was on my right. I walked onto the stadium grounds. A gate was open, so I went in.

The stadium was mostly empty. A few people running the steps. A dad and his son were tossing a football on the field. I remember my dad taking the family to some of the Harvard vs. Yale football games. We would all put on our Harvard sweatshirts, walk to the game, and cheer for the Harvard Crimson. My dad graduated from Harvard and never left Cambridge.

What I wouldn't give to have those carefree days back. But I can't go back. Even if I could, I would end up back here again. Probably just as confused as I am at this very moment.

I went to Italy to teach a summer course at the American Academy. Filling in for my mentor and former professor. The plan was to stay for an additional two weeks as vacation. There was no part of the plan that included meeting a man who would stir such deep feelings within me.

But that is what happened. I met Matteo Rosetti. A chance meeting, actually. Even though I couldn't predict the future, I knew something was going to happen between us. I felt it. He did too. Maybe then it became a self-fulfilling prophecy.

Call it love at first sight. Call it being swept up in the romance of Italy. Call it whatever you want. The fact remains my feelings for Matteo stirred deep within me. They were undeniable. They are feelings not easily dismissed by any amount of time either with him or apart from him.

That one moment of meeting Matteo in the halls of the American Academy changed my life. Our meeting altered the course of my two weeks in Italy. Those two weeks changed my perception of how deeply I could feel for someone.

I would almost say that our meeting was destiny. That Matteo and I were created for each other. Soul mates.

Only I don't know about anything right now. I am supposed to be so smart with all my university degrees. Amanda Evans, PhD. Amanda Evans, newly hired Assistant Professor of Classics at the University of California Los Angeles. Big whoop. I don't have a clue about how to make my love life work.

The man that I have fallen in love with lives a continent and then an ocean away from where I live. There are over 6,300 miles between Los Angeles and Rome. It's too far of an expanse for me to comprehend how we can be a couple.

Now, the man that I once dated has just told me that he still loves me. We only broke up the beginning of the summer.

It was mutual. It was amicable. I loved him once. But not with the depth that I do Matteo. Not even close.

It almost seems ridiculous. I am in love with a man who I only met two weeks ago. Because it is so new and because he is in Italy and I am not, I hesitated in telling Brad about him. But I have to. I need to.

It's not like it is the perfect scenario for Brad and me. I live in California and Brad is now in Massachusetts. I will be teaching at UCLA and Brad is likely to being playing football for the New England Patriots.

He had actually given a lot of thought to how we could make a relationship work. Not perfect, but it could work. Theoretically, at least. Except that I am not in love with him. Oh yeah, there's that little factoid. The problem is that I don't know how to tell him.

I got up and left the stadium. I turned left and retraced my steps along North Harvard Street, across Soldiers Field Road, over the Charles River, along the Anderson Memorial Bridge, and across Memorial Drive. I turned left and continued past John F. Kennedy Park and along Memorial Drive. The park was filled with sunbathers, people flipping Frisbees back and forth, and Kennedy School of Government staff enjoying sack lunches on the benches and lawn.

I continued on toward my parents' house. When I walked through the door my mother anxiously greeted me. "How was your walk?" she asked as she looked around for Brad. "You were gone a long time."

"I was out walking alone for much of it," I replied.

"What happened?" asked Mom.

"Nothing." Okay, I wasn't being totally honest. But I really didn't want to discuss it.

"Is everything okay? Bradley is such a nice young man. Did the two of you have a fight?"

"No. We did not have a fight. Mom, Brad is a great guy. But we are just friends now. We talked. He had to go. I wanted to enjoy the great weather and went for a walk. Nothing else to it."

I don't think that my mother bought it, but she let it go. For now. I knew that she would come back to it later. Her approach would probably lean toward convincing me that Brad and I should get back together.

"We will leave in ten minutes to go visit Tina at Mass General," my mom said.

"Okay. I'm just going to freshen up quickly." I retreated upstairs. At least I would get ten minutes of peace without having to discuss my love life. Or whatever it was at the moment.

CHAPTER 32

The following day, Tina was released from the hospital. We had an afternoon and evening with her at my parents' house. Today, we were taking her to White Mountains Clinic to begin her rehabilitation program.

Holly and I were traveling on I-93 North toward the White Mountains region of New Hampshire. My parents, Scott, and Tina were in my dad's car in front of us. It seemed like we were moving painfully slow as cars zipped past us in the other lanes.

"Dad does know that the speed limit is 65, right?" asked Holly a bit perturbed at traveling ten miles below the speed limit. "It will be 70 once we hit the New Hampshire border."

My parents weren't exactly elderly. But they were a study in contrast. They balked at being old enough to join the association of retired persons when the invitation arrived in the mail last year. My dad had commented that they were only in their mid-50s. Nowhere close to retirement. At the same time, my dad was set in his ways and never adjusted to the change in the speed limit from 55 mph to 65 mph on the highways.

"So pass him and go however fast you want," I suggested.

Holly's nose wrinkled the way that it did when she was concentrating on something.

"It's not like I'm a speed demon or anything, but I'd like to at least go the speed limit. We're being passed like we are sitting still. It's over three hours even at the speed limit." Holly continued.

"So pass him," I said again.

"Then again, I don't want us to get there too much ahead of them."

"We can stop for coffee. I'd rather sit in a coffee shop and take in small town New England than spend more time on the interstate," I said. Rather convincing, I thought. I also didn't want to have a five minute conversation about this. Holly could take my suggestion or leave it. Thankfully, she took it. She nodded her head in agreement. Decision made.

Holly checked her rear-view mirror, gave a glance out her window over her shoulder, put on her left turn signal, pulled into the left lane and accelerated. As we passed the rest of our family in dad's car, I gave a smile and a wave. Fifteen seconds later my cell phone rang. Mom was a little slower on the draw than usual.

"It's Mom," I announced.

"No surprise there," replied Holly with a smirk.

"Hi Mom," I said as I answered.

"Are you girls trying to break some sort of speed record?" my mother asked.

"Mom, the speed limit is 65. It will be 70 in New Hampshire. Holly and I would like more time in the fresh mountain air. We'll stop for coffee or ice cream with the extra time," I said with a smile. I knew that my mom couldn't see me smile, but I figured she could feel it over the cell signal.

"Just don't let Holly get a ticket," she replied.

"Mom, they don't give out tickets for going the speed limit. We'll see you in New Hampshire." I ended our call and dropped my phone into my purse.

"You hadn't suggested ice cream as an option before," said Holly.

"Just thought of it."

"We should consider that. I bet there is a great homemade ice cream shop. It just seems like something we should find where we are going."

"Agreed. We will check on that when we get closer," I said.

"Okay, we need road trip jams," announced Holly.

I flipped through her CD case. I found a CD with her handwriting that was labeled *Holly's Road Trip Jams* in black marker.

"You literally have a CD for that."

"Of course I do."

I popped the disc into the car's player. The first song started playing. I could tell that it would be a collection of upbeat pop hits from Holly's favorite singers. Scott would hate it. It was okay with me.

"Now, tell me more about what happened between you and Brad," said Holly.

I had started to tell her about what had happened before we were interrupted by our parents to go visit Holly in the hospital. After that it had been non-stop family time. It worked out well that my dad's car would not fit five of us comfortably. Holly and I had an excuse to ride together in Holly's car. Lots of sister time.

"Well, he took me completely by surprise," I began. "He told me how much he missed me and how great we had been together. Then, he started talking about how really great we could still be together. That he wanted to get back together."

"Really? He wants you two to start dating again?"

"Yes. It was clear that he had been thinking a lot about it. Even what my objections might be. You know, how he would be here playing for the Patriots and I will be teaching at UCLA."

"That long-distance relationships do not work," said Holly.

"Exactly. He told me that given the football schedule, we would only really be apart for the fall semester."

Holly thought about that for a moment. "I guess I could see that," she said. "Training camp is in August, the regular season lasts until the end of December. The Patriots are usually in the playoffs, so January. If they reach the Super Bowl, the beginning of February. So, he is pretty close."

"When did you become such an expert on the football season?" I asked. "We never gave it any thought growing up. Even with Dad and Scott following every Boston sports team."

"It helps me connect with the kids in my class," she replied. "But that isn't what is important right now. Tell me more. I need the details."

"Okay, so he made the case that we would have all spring and most of the summer together. Plus, he would fly me to wherever the games were being played for any weekends I wanted to see him during the season."

"I guess he had thought it through."

"Then he told me that he still loves me."

"What?!" Holly looked over at me.

"Keep your eyes on the road," I said. "Yes. He said that he still loves me."

"Wow. What did you say?"

"Nothing."

"Nothing? Your ex-boyfriend, who is super cute and a really nice guy, says that he is still in love with you and you say nothing?" Holly was incredulous.

"I didn't literally say nothing. But I didn't really give him an answer either. I was caught off guard. I stammered on about how I wasn't expecting that, and how he would always have a place in my heart, but that I wasn't sure about being in love with him, . . ."

"Do you still have feelings for him?" asked Holly.

"Yes. And no," I replied. "Brad is a wonderful guy. We were great together. I did love him. I suppose, on some level, I still do. I just never considered our relationship as particularly long term. I didn't think he had either."

"Why did you dismiss it as being a potentially long term relationship?"

"I suppose it just seemed easier that way. It didn't seem likely that we were headed in the same direction in our lives. We were almost certain to be in different cities. Different professional schedules."

"So it would have been hard?"

"Yes."

"But not impossible?"

"That's not fair," I said a bit defensively.

"Touchy, touchy," replied Holly.

"Brad had said that he had thought about us being long term."

"And he never told you that when you were dating?"

"No. He said yesterday that he got the distinct impression that I was not thinking long term about us. So he never went there."

"You can be pretty headstrong," observed Holly.

"I know." I couldn't really argue the point. I wondered if I would be like my parents thirty years from now. Resisting the senior discount card and being set in my ways over speed limits and a host of other things? I sighed.

"What are you going to do?" asked Holly.

"I don't know," I replied. "I still can't let go of the idea of being with Matteo."

"Your Italian romance?"

"Don't say it like that," I retorted.

"So this is more about how you feel about Matteo?"

"I guess so."

"It's not my life," said Holly, "and I am your younger sister, but I don't see how you can consider being with Matteo. He's in Italy. He's staying in Italy. He is moving on and said you should do the same. You are just about to start your career at UCLA. Which is in California. Like, what, 6,000 miles from Italy?"

"I know the obstacles."

"Amanda, I love you, you are my sister. You are also one of my very best friends in the entire world. I think it is great that you are getting to live your dream, as nerdy as it might be, of being a classics professor. But let's face it, there isn't a huge demand for someone with a PhD in Classics. There is no way you can even consider throwing what you have away. Not for a guy you spent two weeks with while on vacation in another country. It just doesn't make any sense."

"I know all of that, too," I said. "But sometimes life gives you something that makes sense even when it doesn't."

"Huh? I don't follow."

"Matteo and I were so right together. It broke my heart to leave him and return home. I felt like a left a huge piece of me with him in Italy. I know that it doesn't look like there is any realistic way for us to be together right now, but I don't think I can give up all hope. Not yet."

"Is that what you are going to tell Brad?"

"I think that it is the only thing that I can tell him. It may be confusing as heck, but it is the truth."

"And then what?"

"I'm still trying to figure that part out."

CHAPTER 33

We decided on ice cream. The town where White Mountains Clinic is located had a local ice cream shop. After we had Tina settled into her room at the clinic, there would be lunch with my parents, Scott, and Holly. That would be followed by another three-hour car ride back to Cambridge. It wasn't alone time, but I hoped that I might gain some clarity on what to do. Even if I was thinking about it in the background of my mind.

The White Mountains Clinic was an old farmhouse that had been remodeled on the inside. It retained much of the original farmhouse charm, but was clearly no longer a single family home. The downstairs still had the living room as communal space, and the dining room was expanded to accommodate clinic participants. There were a dozen small, private, bedrooms upstairs.

Tina's room for the next several weeks had a single bed, dresser, chair and lamp for reading, a small desk for journal writing, and a private bathroom. Everything was basic, but had a New England country charm. The clinic was welcoming and comfortable.

The director of the clinic went over the daily schedule and asked if we had any questions about the rehabilitation program. They had a very impressive success rate of addicts being able to conquer their addictions and live healthy and productive lives. That was certainly our hope for Tina.

We were all thrilled to see Tina seeming relaxed and committed to the clinic's program. "I like it here," she told us. "I think this will be very good for me."

"We want you to get fully better," my mom said to Tina. "We love you and want you to be healthy and happy." She wiped a small tear from her eye. My dad handed her a facial tissue.

"I want that too," said Tina. "Maybe for the first time in a long time."

We took turns hugging Tina and saying goodbye. The rest of my family would be back for visits on weekends. I would be leaving for California and would only be able to talk to Tina by phone.

"I'll call every week," I told her. Tina nodded her head and smiled. "I'd like that," she told me. We hugged again before she left to have lunch with other program participants. We watched her go into the dining room and then we left.

My mother was tearing up a bit more by the time we reached the parking lot. Mixed emotions. Sadness at having Tina away for several weeks. Happy, and relieved, that Tina was going to get the help that she needed. My dad tried to lighten the mood by suggesting that we have lunch at the little family restaurant on Main Street. "It looked like good, regular, fare," he said.

"As long as I can get a burger, I'm good," said Scott. We all agreed that the restaurant looked fine. Five minutes later, we were seated at a table in Bartlett's Family Restaurant. It had a country kitchen feel to it. The food smelled great, and the staff were friendly. We ordered and then my mom started in on me.

"It was so nice seeing Bradley," she said. Her way of opening the conversation to the many reasons why I should start dating Brad again.

I kept my reply short and sweet. "Yes, it was," I said.

"He is such a nice young man. I always liked him," my mom continued. "So handsome."

I tried to ignore my mother by looking at my menu. "What looks good to everyone?" I said, trying to shift the focus of the conversation.

"You're right. We can discuss this after we order," said my mom.

"Or, we can let Amanda have a personal life," offered Holly.

"Holly Irene Evans," said my mom. Irene was my paternal grandmother. Rose was my maternal grandmother. Tina got a great aunt's name, Rebecca, for her middle name. Scott had my dad's name, Robert, for his middle name. "We are family. That is personal," continued my mom.

"All I am saying is that Amanda deserves to have a little privacy when it comes to her love life. Or whether she even has a love life with any particular person," said Holly.

"What is that suppose to mean? Is Amanda not interested in Brad?" asked my mom.

"Hello, sitting right here," I said as I waved my hand in front of me.

"Well?" asked my mom as she looked directly at me.

"Holly is sort of right, Mom. I'm twenty-seven years old. I do, believe it or not, make many of my own decisions. Including who I date."

"I wasn't suggesting that you didn't. All I am saying is that you should feel free to discuss it with your family."

"And I do. When I choose to."

"Brenda, how about the grilled chicken sandwich? It looks wonderful," my dad said trying to defuse the situation.

"Okay, okay," said my mom. "I get the hint. Butt out."

"It's not like that, Mom. It's just . . . I don't see a future with Brad. I'm not sure that there is more to say than that at the moment."

"Well, you could do a lot worse. But, message received," said Mom. She started looking at her menu. Then she tried to lay on a bit of a guilt trip. Not just on me. On all three Evans kids at the table. "It would be nice to have grandchildren."

"Maybe the pot roast?" said my dad.

Thankfully the waitress came and took our order. Scott then shifted the conversation to the book he was starting to write on wages in the U.S. Economy. I was happy to discuss anything other than my love life. All I had to do was navigate away from that topic for another day before I left for Los Angeles. Easier said than done.

CHAPTER 34

Holly dropped me off at my parents and then headed back to her apartment in Newton. Scott was going home as well. He had an apartment in Chestnut Hill, not far from where he taught at Boston College. We said goodbye, and he wished me luck for my first academic year as a professor. My parents and I ordered a pizza for dinner and watched a movie on Netflix.

My mom didn't press me any further on Brad, my overall love life, or about getting married and having children. I was especially impressed as I told them that I had made dinner plans with Brad for the following evening. I slept well and woke up refreshed. I had a lite breakfast with my parents and we took a long walk together along the Charles River.

Crew teams were rowing on the river. The sidewalk was busy with joggers, bikers, and others out for a leisurely summer stroll. When we got back to the house my dad put on the Red Sox game. Mom and I went out to lunch and to do some shopping. When we got home from shopping, I went upstairs to get most of my packing out of the way.

I called Jenny to make sure she could still pick me up from the airport the next day. We ended up talking for an hour. I avoided any discussion about Brad or Matteo. It was just chit chat. That is what I needed.

I padded downstairs at about 5:45. "I'm heading out now," I announced to my parents.

"Have a nice dinner, dear," said my mom. "Say hello to Brad for us."

"I will. See you in a few hours," I said. I ducked out the door and got away with no further discussion about Brad.

I walked to Harvard Square and met Brad at the Border Cafe. I loved their Tex-Mex food. Brad seemed a bit apprehensive at first. I think he knew that this dinner would be two friends rather than former boyfriend and girlfriend who were getting back together.

As we entered the restaurant I could hear the sizzle of fajitas as the sweet and spicy aroma filled the air. I could picture the steam rising off the hot steak or chicken as they were piled on the hot black griddles. We were seated at a table near the window. One of my favorite spots. People passed by on Church Street just outside the window. I missed living in Cambridge.

Brad seemed to read my mind. "Maybe one day you will teach at Harvard and can move back to Cambridge," he said.

"I think I would really have to set myself apart in the field to be offered a position on the Harvard faculty. But it is a nice thought."

"You can do it. You have always been able to do anything you put your mind to," Brad said with a smile.

"You're very sweet. Perhaps a little delusional, but sweet." We shared a good laugh, and that seemed to ease Brad a bit. The waitress came over. We ordered Gucomoli as an appetizer. I got a Strawberry Margarita and Brad ordered a Corona. We went ahead and put in our dinner order as well. Fajitas for both of us. Chicken for me and steak for Brad.

"Amanda, I don't want tonight to be awkward between us. I know what I said the other day and that it must have seemed like it was out of the blue. I meant what I said, but I know that it is a lot for you to think about."

"It is a lot for me to think about. And I have given it a lot of thought . . ."

"Why do I have the feeling that you are letting me down gently?"

I offered a slight smile, but turned my gaze down toward the table for a few seconds.

"Okay. I get it," continued Brad. "You don't have to say anything."

"But I should say something. Brad, you are an amazing guy. I do love you. I always will. I just don't think that I am ready to be in love with you right now. My love life is pretty confusing at the moment. I met this guy in Italy and . . ."

"You don't have to explain it to me," said Brad. "I really do understand. We broke up as friends. We saw each other as friends the other day. We are still friends now. I'd be lying if I said that I didn't want more, but you mean too much to me not to have you in my life."

Our drinks and appetizer came. I took a good sip of my margarita. Brad pushed the lime wedge into the bottle of Corona.

"To a great friend," Brad said as held up the bottle. I held up my glass. "To an amazing friend," I said. We smiled and took a sip of our drinks. Maybe if I hadn't met Matteo this would be going differently. Then again, if Brad and I were meant to be together, we probably wouldn't have broken up in the first place.

I guess there is no way of knowing for sure. Past decisions were just that. But we are where we are at because of them. The future is still to be realized, but I could already see that there were two possible outcomes for me. Matteo and I would find a way to be together, or we wouldn't. I could only see a future with Brad that included being dear friends.

Dinner was fantastic. Considering that the evening could have been a total disaster for us, Brad and I had a nice time together. I certainly did. All indications were that he did as well. And I think I knew him well enough to be a pretty good judge on whether he was having a good time.

After dinner, Brad gave me a kiss on the cheek and told me to have a safe trip back to Los Angeles. I wished him luck at training camp and asked him to let me know how it went. He again promised to get my family tickets to a game if he made the team. We hugged. Brad headed for the subway and I walked back to my parents' house.

I wondered if I would ever have the opportunity to walk through Harvard Square with Matteo as we visited my parents. Or maybe my family would visit us in Italy. Was there a scenario where I could move to Italy? Probably not. It would be hard for an American with a doctorate in Classics to compete with an Italian that had the same degree. They had the home field advantage. Not just in citizenship, but of breathing the same air as the ancients we study, research, and teach about.

I made my turn off Brattle Street. I walked another block and made another turn onto the street where I had grown up. The only home that I knew until I left for college. I had now lived in Los Angeles nine years. Four years undergrad and five years getting my PhD. All at USC. Now I was moving a little across the city to UCLA to teach. But LA was home now. I figured that is where I would be building my future. With or without Matteo in it.

CHAPTER 35

My carry-on bag was flung over my shoulder and I was pulling my suitcase behind me. I scanned the pickup area in front of the terminal for Jenny's car. I had just hung up with her. She had described that she was pulled over between a maroon SUV and a black Towne Car. There were several black Towne Cars from various car services, so that made the task a little harder. I spotted the maroon SUV and saw Jenny waving to me. I moved through the crowd on the sidewalk and reached Jenny's car.

"It is so great to have you home," Jenny said with a big hug.

"It is nice to be home." I put my suitcase in her trunk and slammed it shut. I hopped in the passenger side.

"How was your flight?" asked Jenny was we moved into the flow of traffic that was exiting LAX.

"It was fine. I just zoned out and watched the satellite TV and read a bit. Then I took a nap."

"I can never sleep on planes," said Jenny.

We exited the airport and traveled on California Route 1 North toward the University of Southern California. I was still living in my graduate student apartment just off campus. I would need to find a new place to live, and fast.

"Do you want to help me look at apartments this weekend?" I asked Jenny.

"That could be fun. When do you have to be out of your current place?"

"The end of next week."

"The end of next week? And you are waiting to look now?"

"I wasn't planning on spending nearly a week in Boston after Italy."

"Amanda, that still would have given you only two weeks to find a place and move."

"I'm sure there are enough places available. Besides, what is there to move? It was a furnished student apartment. I only have a few boxes of personal stuff and clothes. It will all fit in my car."

Jenny just shook her head. I knew what she was thinking. And it was true. As nerdy, organized, and driven as I am in my academic and professional life, I tend to do things rather last minute when it comes to my personal life. Nonetheless, it always seems to work out for me. If it 'aint broke why fix it?

"I will definitely help you look for an apartment. We should start early in the morning. No time to waste. I assume you will want to be close to UCLA?"

"Yes to being as close to UCLA as possible. But do we have to start looking early in the morning? I know your definition of early."

"I was thinking 10:00 AM," replied Jenny.

I was relieved. Jenny is one of those morning persons. I am not.

"Most of the apartment complexes don't start showings until ten," Jenny informed me.

"Ten is fine."

"Okay, enough of that. Get me caught up on everything," she said.

Jenny slowed the car and then stopped. We were stuck in traffic. I only live five miles from the airport. That is about fourteen minutes without a traffic delay. But it is LA. There is almost always a traffic delay. I read somewhere that Los Angelenos spend 34% more time in their cars than the average American driver.

"Well, let's see. You know about Tina's trip to the hospital and my family getting her into rehab. The clinic is very nice. I actually think she will do well there. She seems committed in a way that I don't think she ever has been."

"I am glad to hear that," said Jenny as she inched the car forward with the snails paced flow of traffic. "I know that you wanted to keep our conversation easy going on the phone yesterday, but what is going on with Brad? I can't believe your mom invited him over for breakfast."

"I did leave out the most important parts."

"Okay. Like what?"

"Like he told me that he was still in love with me and wanted to get back together."

"What?!"

"Yeah. I know. He took me completely by surprise with that. We ended our relationship as friends. Our break up was mutual and amicable. I figured we would remain friends. But friends who kept in touch over Facebook and email, and such. I was not at all prepared for him wanting to get back together."

"So, what happened? Are you getting back together? Ooh, it would be a long distance relationship. I'm guessing probably not. To getting back together."

"Jenny, that made my head hurt. A lot going on there. But, to answer your questions, no. We are definitely not getting back together. He took it well though. We are still friends."

We moved forward another few inches. Brake lights ahead of us as far as the eye could see. Jenny looked disappointed.

I'm sure it had more to do with the fact that I had not slept with Brad than the traffic conditions. She spent more time in LA traffic than I did. I had always lived on or very near USC's campus.

"Still thinking about your handsome Italian boyfriend?"

"Don't call Matteo that. But, yes."

"Sweetie, you need to let it go. Time to move on."

"It has only been a week."

"And you only spent two weeks with him. How long does it take to get over a two week romance that had little chance of being anything more?"

"I don't know. I've never had the experience before Matteo. And it is not that simple. Yes, it was only two weeks. Jenny, I've tried to tell you before that the feelings and the connection between us was amazing. I think it was love at first sight. A love that was reinforced over those two weeks."

"Okay. But does that change the fact he is staying in Italy? Your life is here. In Los Angeles."

"Perhaps."

"Alright. So maybe all you need is time. The school year starts soon. An exciting new adventure awaits you as Amanda Evans, Assistant Professor. And I'll be sure that we double up on our girls nights out."

"Thanks." I appreciated Jenny. She had been my best friend since Freshman year in college. I loved her like a sister. I was as close to Jenny as I was Holly. In some ways, maybe even closer. Nonetheless, I knew that there was much more going on than simply needing more time.

I was in love with Matteo. The feelings for him were stronger than I had ever felt for anyone. As we sat in the car, barely going anywhere, I thought of Matteo's olive skin, wavy dark hair, piercing dark eyes, and full lips.

"Amanda? Did you hear me?" asked Jenny as she looked over at me.

"Huh? What? No, I'm sorry. What did you say?"

"I know that look. You were thinking about Mr. Italy. Weren't you?"

"Let's drop it. What were you saying?"

"I was asking you if you wanted to take a look at some apartment sites online tonight and figure out which ones to check out in person tomorrow?"

"Yes. That sounds like a good idea." Anything to take my mind off of how much I missed Matteo.

CHAPTER 36

Jenny and I spent two hours looking at apartment websites. There were several good options for me, but I hadn't found exactly what I wanted. I had applied for faculty housing in one of the university owned apartments off-campus, but there was nothing available. I put my name on the wait list in hopes that I might get something next year.

There were a number of apartments in the UCLA area, but rents are pretty high in Los Angeles. As a brand new assistant professor, and in a lower paying field, I was at the minimum faculty salary. I'm not complaining, though. I'm starting out debt free. My parents had paid for my tuition to USC as an undergraduate and I had department funding for my graduate studies. I drove a fifteen year old car that I had bought used when I left for college. All the same, a sizable portion of my income would go toward housing. That limited what I could consider.

When I met Jenny the following morning, I had the list of places that I had decided on from our work the night before. I was less than thrilled with the prospect of apartment hunting. I should have been filled with the excitement of finding my first post-student place to live as I began my career. Instead, it seemed much more like a task to complete. My heart just wasn't in it. In any of it.

Jenny opened the door to her apartment. She took one look at me and handed me a cup of coffee in a travel mug. "You look like you really need this," she said. Jenny knew I wasn't a morning person and that I would function much better if I was fueled by caffeine. It's the little things that add up and account for so much in a friendship. Jenny is an A+ BFF.

"Thanks." I took the cup of coffee from Jenny and feigned a smile. Jenny pulled the door shut behind her.

"What's wrong?" she asked as we walked to my car.

"I'm just not feeling it," I said. "I know that I should be excited. Starting my career and finding a place to live . . ."

"Amanda, I know that you are in the doldrums about Matteo. It is okay to be bummed about the situation. You want to talk about it?"

"Not really. I'm not sure there is anything else to say. There certainly isn't anything more that can be done right now. I just need him in a way that I have never really needed anyone before."

"Just trying to help."

"It is appreciated. It is just that I am having a hard time letting go. I don't want to move on. I'm not ready to give up hope of being with him again. And actually not being with him is driving me crazy. Jenny, I've not gotten this worked up over a guy before. Not even Brad."

"Okay, I get it. I know that I have been encouraging you to appreciate it for what it was and move on. But you seem much more hung up on him than I originally thought. You really have some strong feelings for him, huh?"

"Jenny, I'm in love with him. I think I felt it from the moment we met. Like we were destined to meet. As I got to know him . . . it was like I had found my soul mate. He became that much a part of me in that short time."

"In love with him? Are you sure?"

I nodded my head very emphatically. "Yes. Maybe I am crazy for falling for him so hard and so fast, but . . ."

"It is the way you feel. Amanda, your feelings are your feelings. No one can tell you not to feel a certain way. Besides, it's not like there is some timetable for falling in love."

I asked, "So you don't think I am totally nuts?"

"Not totally," said Jenny.

I smiled and gave her a hug. "You truly are the best." I said.

"Okay. So you are in love with Matteo. You need to be with him then. How do we make that happen?"

"That is what I have been turning over in my mind since before I even left Italy."

"Maybe he can come for a visit. You could probably spend the summer in Italy. That is a great thing about being a college professor; summers off. I know it isn't perfect, but it would be something. At least for now. Who knows what options might exist a year from now."

"I guess you're right," I said. "I have been so focused on the fact that Matteo wasn't moving to LA that I didn't consider how we might find ways to be together. At least for a few months at a time. Then there is my winter break. That's another month."

"See. We just came up with the possibility of five or six months out of the year where you can be together. Not the ideal situation, but if the alternative is never seeing him again—"

"Which I don't want to do."

"Then it is an option."

"Have I told you lately what an amazing best friend you are?" I asked.

Jenny acted like she was pondering the question. Then she smiled and wrapped her arms around me in a giant hug. "You just did. And the feeling is mutual."

"Hold on a second," I said as my phone vibrated in my back pocket. I was super casual and traveling lite without a purse. I glanced at the screen. A local number, but one that I did not recognize. I debated whether I should answer. Curiosity got the better of me.

"Hello," I said.

"Professor Evans, this is Anna Rodriguez from the UCLA housing office. Sorry to bother you on a Saturday."

"Not at all. It is no bother. I'm just surprised that you are working on a Saturday."

"It is always crazy just before the start of the new academic year. Between student and faculty housing . . . at any rate, I am calling because your name was at the top of our wait list. A condo has opened up at Village Terrace. The professor who has lived there just informed us that he has purchased a house. If you are still interested, you could actually take a look at it this weekend."

"Yes. I am definitely still interested. This is great news. My friend and I were just about to go look at places. Any chance that I could see it today?"

"Certainly. The building manager is on site until three this afternoon. If you know what time you want to visit, I can call and set the appointment for you."

"How about in the next hour?"

"Okay. I will set up the appointment. It is a nice unit. I think you will like it."

"Thank you so much."

"My pleasure. Have a nice weekend and I hope it works out for you."

"Thank you. Have a great day."

We hung up and Jenny already had the gist of what was going on. I filled her in on the details. An hour later we toured the condo.

I absolutely fell in love with the unit. It was a one bedroom on the third floor. There was a fireplace in the living room and the dining area had a large atrium window that overlooked the city. It had fairly updated appliances and a stacked washer and dryer in the unit. Best of all, it was walking distance to campus.

"It's on the high end of what I can afford. But with water, trash, cable, and internet provided, I can certainly make it work. I'll take it," I told the building manager.

"Excellent. We can go down to my office to sign the lease," he replied.

I had started the day feeling pretty bummed. Jenny usually had a way to make me feel better. She helped me realize that, while my situation with Matteo was not ideal, all was not lost. I even was feeling excited about where I was going to live. The condo was perfect for me. If only Matteo could move to LA, or I could move my condo and my job to Rome.

CHAPTER 37

I spoke with Matteo and we agreed for him to come visit during my Thanksgiving break. At first he was hesitant, fearing it would be too difficult on us both, but I discussed the plan I had hatched with Jenny. While far from ideal, we were both miserable not being together.

Matteo and I had an amazing week together around Thanksgiving. He was so excited to tour Hollywood. We had arranged for a private, behind-the-scenes, tour of Pacific Coast Pictures.

Even though Matteo had not won the internship, the director had been very impressed with his work. When he learned Matteo would be touring the studio, he invited him to lunch. During lunch he asked if Matteo would be interested in working on a big production thriller that takes place in Rome and the surrounding countryside.

Matteo was hired to provide location scouting and serve as an assistant to the film's director. It was a huge opportunity for his film career. And if all went well, there would be more projects. Pacific Coast Pictures was opening a studio in Europe.

I spent Christmas at my parents. Tina was out of rehab and doing great. She was the happiest and most grounded I had ever seen her. She had a new job that she loved and was dating a guy in her office. A really nice guy who treated her well.

Brad made the Patriots. He treated us all to their final regular season game. He caught two touchdown passes. Brad also caught the heart of Holly. They were now dating and I couldn't have been happier for the two of them. Holly's students also thought it was very cool that she was dating a new sports star.

I spent my winter break in Rome. And I went with exciting news that offered hope for a long term relationship with Matteo. In early December I had received a faculty-wide email from the President of UCLA. It was an announcement that the university had just signed an agreement to establish a small international campus in Rome. There would be several subject areas offered. They were listed in alphabetical order. The third subject on the list was *Classical Studies*.

I couldn't believe it. They were looking for UCLA faculty in the selected fields who were interested in applying for the tenure-track faculty positions. I immediately was on the phone with the chair of my department. She knew my situation and fully supported my applying. Decisions would be made by the end of the current academic year.

At the beginning of May I was offered the position of Associate Professor of Classical Studies for the UCLA Rome campus. I would miss Jenny to pieces, but we both knew that I needed to be with Matteo. He was, after all, my Italian love. The love of my life, really.

I moved to Rome in June. I thought back to when Matteo and I had met almost a year ago. We had obstacles in our way, but we persevered. We held tight to our love.

I closed my eyes as Matteo held me close in his arms. I remembered our trip to Venice last summer. "*This is the Sotoportego dei Preti,*" he had informed me. "*Legend has it that if a couple touches the heart together that they will have eternal love.*" We had touched that heart in hopes that it would change the fortunes of our relationship.

I don't know about legends of eternal love. But I know the life I am living. A life I now share in Rome with Matteo. Here's to true love.

****

Want more Sweet Romance Books?
Visit elliejadamsauthor.com for a complete list of all my books.

Newsletter

Join my Newsletter and receive a Sweet Romance story as my gift to you. You will also receive author updates, new release alerts, and exclusive contests and discounts. Free to Join. No Spam. Unsubscribe Anytime. Join at www.elliejadamsauthor.com

Books by Ellie J. Adams

For a complete list of my Sweet Romance books, visit:
www.elliejadamsauthor.com

About the Author

Ellie J. Adams's books have been downloaded over half-a-million times by readers around the world. She is a romantic at heart and likes her characters to find their Happily Ever After. Ellie's books offer moments of drama, humor, and heartache along the way. Her leading men are strong, but flawed, males, and the leading women are sweet, smart, and independent. Ellie writes sweet romance you can get swept up in and takes you away.